Notebooks
of a Middle-school
PRINCESS
BRIDESMAID-IN-TRAINING

Written and illustrated by

MEG CABOT

MACMILLAN CHILDREN'S BOOKS

First published in the US 2016 as *Royal Wedding Disaster* by Feiwel and Friends

First published in the UK 2016 as *Bridesmaid-in-Training* by
Macmillan Children's Books
an imprint of Pan Macmillan
20 New Wharf Road, London N1 9RR
Associated companies throughout the world
www.panmacmillan.com

ISBN 978-1-4472-9248-7

1 3 5 7 9 8 6 4 2

A CIP catalogue record for this book is available from
the British Library.

Saturday 13 June
4.00 p.m.
Royal Genovian Gardens
High Tea

Hi, Olivia! Is everything OK? I know it must be super stressful getting ready for your sister's wedding, but I'm coming there this week (!!!) and you haven't texted me back about how many bathing suits I should bring.

My mom says 5 is too many. But I don't want to be unstylish in Genovia, especially around all those royals and celebrities.

I really hope you aren't mad at me or anything and that's why you haven't written back. Did I do something wrong? OK, well, write back soon (if you aren't mad)!!! ☺ ☺ ☺ Nishi

Oh no. My best friend, Nishi, thinks we're in a fight or something.

But that's not why I haven't texted her in so long. I've just been really super busy. It's no joke, training to be a princess. I've barely had time to write in this notebook, let alone text!

Of course, it hasn't exactly been horrible, either. Not to sound like I'm bragging or anything, but things have been going really *SUPER GREAT.*

And it's not just because I:

1. Get to live in a castle that has its own throne room and ballroom and private library filled with about fifty thousand books (not exaggerating).

2. Have a completely brand-new wardrobe and my own room with orange trees outside my

windows and a private bathroom and a walk-in closet with a couch inside it where I can sit while my personal style consultant, Francesca, figures out what I'm going to wear (only on the days when I have state functions, though. Francesca says it's important not to wear the same thing twice in a row, or it 'disappoints the populace').

3. Get to live in Genovia, which is a tiny country between Italy and France along the Mediterranean Sea, which has white sand beaches and really nice weather year-round.

No! Although that stuff really is pretty awesome. The reason things are going so great is because I finally get to live with people who *actually care about me*.

Now, when I come down to breakfast in the morning, my dad and Grandmère and my sister, Mia, and her fiancé, Michael, ask how I slept, and what I'd like to eat, and what I'm going to do today, and things like that.

My aunt and uncle and cousins back in New

Jersey never *once* asked me any of that stuff. They never cared whether I wanted cereal or French toast or waffles or pancakes or asked me how I liked my eggs. They never even gave me a choice! All we ever got for breakfast back at my old house was oatmeal. Not because they were poor or anything, but because oatmeal is low in fat and high in fibre.

'Oats are nature's broom.' That's what my aunt always used to say.

'Oats?' Grandmère said when I told her this. 'Oats are for horses!'

Ha! I know this is true because as part of my princess lessons, I'm learning how to horseback ride. Dad even got me my very own pony (I was never allowed to have pets at my old house because my aunt didn't want the carpets getting dirty, but now I have a poodle puppy, Snowball, *and* a pony).

The pony's name is Lady Christabel de Champaigne, but I call her Chrissy for short. Chrissy is tan all over, except for her mane and tail, which are gold coloured. When I'm grooming Chrissy — I love to brush her — she makes happy puffing noises with her mouth.

I'm not saying that everything is perfect, of course. Nothing is perfect, not even being a princess and having people love you and living in a palace in the Mediterranean with orange trees outside your bedroom window.

Like right now, for instance, Grandmère and Mia are having another one of their ~~fights~~. (Sorry, I mean disagreements. Grandmère says royals never fight. They have 'disagreements'.)

This disagreement is about Mia's royal wedding, which is exactly one week away.

'No, Grandmère,' Mia is saying. 'I told you before. No purple.'

'But purple is the colour of royalty, Amelia. And it's a *royal* wedding.'

'It's a *summer* wedding in a palace next to the beach. Purple is too dark. Besides, the dresses have already been delivered, and they're cream coloured, just like I asked. We can't change them now.'

'Can't we, Amelia?' Grandmère asked. 'There's such a thing as *dye*, you know.'

'Grandmère,' Mia said. 'My bridesmaids' gowns are cream coloured. And that is final.'

Oh! Mia looks mad. But then, so does Grandmère.

There've been a *lot* of disagreements like this, especially since the wedding is going to be on television and shown worldwide. Five hundred people, including some of the world's most well-known celebrities and royals, have been invited. There's barely room for all the wedding gifts that have already arrived and are on display in the Great Hall.

There are some pretty cool gifts:

- A solid-gold decorated ostrich egg from Australia
- A two-hundred-piece tea set from China
- Silver plates from the people of Austria
- A Moroccan-style crystal-encrusted pet bed for Mia's cat, Fat Louie, from the royal family of Qatar

- And a charitable donation in Mia's and Michael's names to Doctors Without Borders from the president of the United States!

(Personally I don't think charitable donations are a very interesting gift, but donations are what Mia and Michael asked for.)

But here's a secret that almost no one knows, and why there's been so much ~~fighting~~ disagreeing around the palace:

Almost nothing is ready.

It's true! You would think that in a palace that is used to putting on state functions for hundreds of guests, everything would run like clockwork.

But that doesn't turn out to be the case when you're talking about a royal wedding for five hundred that had to be moved up several months because it turns out the bride is having twins.

That's right: I'm going to be an aunt! I went from basically having no family to having SO MUCH FAMILY.

I'm pretty excited about this. I'm especially excited because I get to help pick out the names. The names I've chosen are:

Girl Names	Boy Names
Minnie	Cecil
Vivian	Roberto
Genevieve	Julian
Yvette	Steve

Mia and Michael won't say yet which names they've chosen (they don't even know if the babies are girls or boys).

But Michael keeps joking that if they're boys, he's going to call them Han and Solo (although Mia says she doesn't think this is very funny, and I agree. Naming your baby is serious business, especially if they're in line to a throne).

Anyway, all this hurried-up wedding planning means that in addition to the thousand tourists we get inside the palace every day (it's open for public tours every day from 10 a.m. to 5 p.m., except on Sundays and national holidays), we've also been getting huge amounts of:

Florists, landscapers, stylists, decorators, designers, dressmakers, bakers, musicians, photographers, electricians, builders, contractors, caterers and television studio executives, all running around, trying to get everything ready in time for the Big Day.

But since Mia is what Grandmère calls 'hormonal' — and my dad calls 'stressed' — whenever anyone asks her a wedding-related question, she just goes, 'Pick whatever. I'm sure it will be great.'

But other times — like with the colour of the bridesmaid dresses — she *totally* has an opinion. And it's usually a very boring one, because she doesn't want anyone to make a fuss.

But you HAVE to make fuss over a ROYAL WEDDING. That's the whole point of being a princess bride!

'It's because your sister is a Taurus,' Grandmère says. 'The Taurus is the bull of the astrological signs, and bulls are loyal but stubborn, which makes them strong leaders but absolutely terrible brides.'

I wouldn't know. I'm a Sagittarius. Sagittarians always look on the bright side.

And my dad is 'no help,' according to Grandmère, not only because he's 'a man' and weddings 'scare men' (although I don't think this is true of *all* men; Michael doesn't seem very scared), but because he decided to retire as prince so he could spend more quality time with me, since he missed out on so many of my 'formative years' already.

Except now he's super busy having the summer palace renovated so I can go live in it with him, Mia's little brother, Rocky, and Rocky and Mia's mom, Helen Thermopolis, who Dad says he's going to marry as soon as the summer palace is finished. That way we can 'leave Mia to rule and enjoy being a new bride and mother in peace'.

But it turns out it's going to take months and months to renovate the summer palace because it's nearly five hundred years old and the whole place is sinking into the ground because the foundation is rotten, which Grandmère says is 'ironic'.

I don't really care, though, because until it's fixed, I get to keep living here in the main palace with Mia and Michael and Grandmère and Fat Louie and the twins when they're born!

'Honestly, I don't know what your sister would do without us,' Grandmère said to me just this morning while we were in the royal greenhouse, cancelling the teeny boring white roses that Mia had ordered and replacing them with much more beautiful huge purple irises. 'Now that your father has stepped down from the throne, she's so busy consulting with that new prime minister about important matters of state — such as where to house all those refugees from nearby war-torn countries, and what to name that new strain of genetically modified Genovian orange — that she hasn't a moment to herself. I've no doubt your sister will save the country, of course. But we're the ones who are going to save this wedding, Olivia.'

'I know,' I said. 'Right?'

'It is,' Grandmère said, 'a blessing that we're here.'

It totally is! I hope the summer palace *never* gets a new foundation.

So I don't feel bad about writing in my journal or even texting Nishi back while Mia and Grandmère are ~~fighting~~ disagreeing, since they aren't even paying attention to me and I know it's all for Mia's own good, anyway.

OlivGrace >

Of course I'm not mad at you! It's just that things are super busy. I hope you like the colour purple, because that's what we're going to dye the bridesmaid dresses.

I think 5 bathing suits is fine. Remember, there's a pool here AND the beach. Plus, Grandmère says you can never have too many of anything except enemies.

Guess what else??? Grandmère says we have the most important job of the ENTIRE wedding party, because we have to hold up Mia's train as she walks down the aisle. I'm so excited!!! Can't wait to introduce you to Chrissy!!! And everyone else, of course.

Saturday 13 June
5.00 p.m.
Royal Genovian Gardens
High Tea

Nishi finally texted back, but she didn't say what I was expecting her to.

< NishiGirl

> I'm glad things are going OK and you aren't mad at me!

> OK, 5 bathing suits it is.

> I can't wait to see you!!!!!!!

It's going to be so so fun to hold up your sister's train! And meet your pony.

But I don't see how you're going to have any time at all to spend with me when you're going to be so busy starting princess school on Monday.

School? Who said anything about school?

I think Nishi must be confused. Grandmère and Mia give me princess lessons every day so I won't embarrass myself (or the rest of the family) at the wedding or in front of the paparazzi who follow us around every time we leave the palace, trying to get a photo of 'the princess bride'.

I'm getting a princess lesson right now, as a matter of fact, which is the only reason I'm allowed to be writing in my journal during high tea. Everyone thinks I'm taking notes . . . which I am, sort of.

But princess lessons aren't the same as *real* school.

They're still super important, of course. Nobody wants a loser who doesn't have any manners representing their country, even a country as tiny as Genovia (which is only two miles by four miles long).

Then again, I'm sure nobody wants a loser who doesn't know what the capital of France is representing their country, either.

So maybe Nishi is right.

But Dad said I need to take time to adjust to living in a new country (with a new family) before starting at my new school. And even though I've been here a month, I don't feel that I've totally adjusted yet. I don't even know the names of all my cousins or my way around the palace. There are more rooms in this palace than there are days of the month! I haven't even been in them all yet.

Not that I don't think education is valuable. It's important to learn stuff like maths and geography in addition to curtsying and drinking out of the right glass. There were *so* many glasses on the dining table in the Great Hall at the fancy dinner I went to last night in honour of all our out-of-town guests who've started to arrive for the wedding, I couldn't even tell which water glass was mine and which one belonged to the very large man who was sitting next to me. Finally Mia nudged me under the table.

'Olivia,' she whispered. 'Do this.' She made circles with her index fingers and thumbs and held them in front of her, making the letters *b* and *d*. 'The bread plate on your left — "b" — is yours, and so are the glasses on your right — "d" for drink. Get it?'

I got it, but too late. I'd been drinking out of the very large man's water glass the entire time!

And so was he! *We were drinking out of the same glass.*

Being a princess is *way more* complicated than I ever thought it was going to be.

So given what an embarrassment I already am, it's totally possible they want me to go to some school to learn how to be a better royal . . .

But I don't know. Right now, with the wedding only a week away and Grandmère needing me so much? Something like that, you'd think someone would have mentioned it.

Normally I'm not allowed to look at my phone

during meals — especially high tea! — because Grandmère says it's *extremely rude* not to give your full attention to the person sitting in front of (or beside) you.

'For all you know, Olivia,' Grandmère always says, 'that person could be the leader of a country that is much, *much* bigger than yours.'

'Or,' Mia says, 'they could just be very nice, and you don't want to act like a jerk by sitting there looking at your phone and not paying attention to them.'

But since this seems very important and Grandmère and Mia are still ~~fighting~~ disagreeing over the colour of the bridesmaid dresses, I figured no one would notice if I quickly texted Nishi back. So I wrote:

OlivGrace ＞

What are you talking about? Who told you I'm starting school on Monday? Also, if you mean the Royal Genovian Academy, it's not 'princess school', it's just regular school. Boys go there, too.

W/B soon!

But it's been nearly ten minutes and I haven't heard back.

Which reminds me . . . it's June. No one *starts* a new school in June. That's when school gets out for summer holidays! Nishi got out of school last week!

So she must be wrong. Why would I be starting school now, right when everything is getting busiest with the wedding planning? That would be simply — WHA!!!!!

Saturday 13 June
5.50 p.m.
Royal Genovian Gardens
High Tea

BUSTED.

Nishi texted me back just as I was writing all that, but Grandmère heard the chime and got angry.

'Princesses don't text at tea!' she yelled, startling me so badly that I dropped my phone into a nearby potted hydrangea. Fortunately when I managed to fish it out, I found that the screen wasn't even cracked — well, any more than it already was from when I dropped it a few days before by the pool. So that was all right.

Then Rommel, Grandmère's hairless poodle, started barking, and Grandmère had to divert him with a ham sandwich, even though I've told her a bunch of times that this is why all Rommel's fur has fallen out: Dogs aren't supposed to eat people food.

This caused enough of a distraction from the argument she and Mia were having for me to ask, 'Is it true I have to go to school on Monday?'

'School?' Grandmère raised her painted-on eyebrows very dramatically. 'Don't be ridiculous. Who said anything about school? We're much too busy with your sister's wedding right now to worry about something like *school*.'

'Grandmère,' Mia said severely. 'School is important. Lack of education limits opportunities and prospects, especially for women . . . even princesses.'

'Is that why Nishi just texted me *this*?' I asked, showing them my phone (once I'd brushed the dirt from the screen).

< NishiGirl

There was just a headline on RateTheRoyals.com:

Her Royal Highness Olivia Grace of Genovia will join

'Pfuit!' Grandmère exclaimed after she read the text. *Pfuit* is the noise she makes when she's truly disgusted. '*This* is what passes for news in America? Whatever is the matter with journalists there? Have they nothing to do but focus on us royals? Are there no celebrity couples divorcing at the moment?'

'Grandmère, *please*,' Mia said sternly.

'But how can this even be happening?' I asked. 'How can reporters know about this if *I* don't? It isn't true, is it? No one mentioned anything to *me* about starting school on Monday.'

'Oh dear,' Mia said, looking a little ill. According to Nishi — who spends a lot of time online — this is normal when you're pregnant with twins and suffering from hormones. Only I hope I never get them as bad as Mia, since her hormones cause her to have to run to the royal powder room a *lot*. 'I'm afraid it *is* true, Olivia. With everything going on with the wedding, it completely slipped my mind.'

'*What* slipped your mind?' I could feel myself beginning to panic.

'We got a letter here at the palace last month from Madame Alain, the head of the Royal Genovian Academy. The letter said that if you aren't in class by Monday morning, you'll be considered truant and dropped from the school's enrolment . . . *permanently.*'

WHAT????

'How dare that woman?' Grandmère cried. 'She doesn't have the authority. Doesn't she know who we *are*?'

'Yes, of course she does, Grandmère,' Mia said. 'And Madame Alain is right. She says we're setting a bad example for the rest of the populace by keeping Olivia out of school — unless we're homeschooling her, which of course we aren't.'

'What do you mean?' Grandmère looked angry. 'Olivia's learning valuable *life* lessons by spending her time with me.'

'It's true!' I said. 'Haven't I been doing a good

job at my princess training?' I gasped, remembering last night's dinner. 'Is this because of the water glass?'

'Of course not!' Mia said. 'You've been doing very well, Olivia. But life lessons aren't the same as academics, and Dad and Grandmère and I simply don't have time — or the knowledge — to teach you *everything* you need to know in order to become a well-rounded Genovian citizen.'

Grandmère snorted delicately. 'Speak for yourself, Amelia.'

Mia gave her a pained look. 'Certainly we can teach you deportment and diplomacy. But I meant things like maths, literature and science. And while I know the timing isn't ideal, it probably isn't the worst thing in the world for you to go to school on Monday. Things here at the palace are getting a little . . . well, *hectic*, with all of the guests and television crews and reporters arriving.'

Now *I* felt a little sick. And it wasn't from eating too many tea cakes, either (although I'd eaten quite a few).

'Hectic?' I echoed. 'I think you mean fun!'

Suddenly there was a loud *TWANG!* followed by a *THUNK*.

This was because Grandmère had fired off the bow and arrow she'd stolen from Mia's half-brother, Rocky.

'Drat,' Grandmère said, lowering the bow. 'Missed again.'

'Grandmère, *please.*' Mia dropped her head into her hands. '*Please* stop shooting arrows at the drones.'

One thing no one tells you about being royal (besides the fact that a mean lady is going to force you to go to royal school) is that the paparazzi will basically stop at nothing to try to get a picture of you, even fly drones with cameras over the palace walls. They're *always* doing this, despite the fact that it's against the law.

It's kind of fun to hit the drones with sticks (or towels, if you happen to be by the pool).

But Grandmère likes to shoot at them with

Rocky's bow and arrow. She says she enjoys the exercise, and that it's important to maintain her hand-eye coordination.

'I've told you,' Mia said to Grandmère. 'The Royal Genovian Guard will take care of the drones. We can't have you shooting at them yourself. You're going to hurt someone . . . like my friends, if they ever get back from shopping.'

'Oh, I wasn't shooting at a drone,' Grandmère said matter-of-factly. 'I was shooting at another one of those hideous creatures.'

Mia lifted her head sharply. 'Grandmère! *No!*'

'Well, what else am I to do, Amelia? They're simply ravaging my hibiscus, and I want the garden to look beautiful for your wedding.'

I love animals very much — I want to be a wildlife illustrator some day (if I can do it in between my important work of being a princess).

But iguanas — which Grandmère calls 'those hideous creatures' — are not that cute. There's a kind-of-cute one that hangs out near the orange tree

beneath my bedroom window and is bright green. Since he's just a baby and iguanas don't eat citrus, I don't mind him. I've even named him Carlos.

But the grown-up ones that roam around the Royal Genovian Gardens are bigger than Snowball! And they have long claws, and spikes coming out of their backs, and sometimes they poop right next to the pool or even *in* it, which is not only disgusting but unhealthy and rude.

Still, I don't think Grandmère should be shooting at them, especially with real arrows instead of the rubber-tipped ones Rocky was using to shoot at the busts in the Hall of Portraits (which is how he got his bow taken away from him by his mother in the first place).

Fortunately for the iguanas — especially Carlos — Grandmère has pretty terrible aim.

So this particular arrow went sailing harmlessly into the blue-and-white-striped cushion of one of the pool loungers, instead of into the iguana.

But not before it almost hit one of the footmen in the leg.

'I do beg your pardon, André,' Grandmère said to the footman as he returned her arrow.

'I quite understand, Your Highness,' André said with a bow. 'I find the iguanas a nuisance as well.'

'It isn't the iguanas' fault.' I felt I should remind them. 'Dad says they aren't even from around here. Someone must have let a caged pair go, and somehow they ended up here in the Royal Genovian Gardens, where they had babies, and then the babies had babies, and now there are hundreds of iguanas everywhere, having even more babies.'

'Yes!' Grandmère cried. 'And eating all of my hibiscus!'

'They're herbivores, Grandmère,' Mia said. 'Flowers are all that iguanas eat. And if Genovia can make room for all of the refugees, certainly we can make room for a few iguanas.'

'The refugees don't go to the bathroom in my pool, Amelia,' Grandmère said. 'And we can't have lizards dropping down from the trees on top of people's heads during your wedding reception. Everyone will think they've stepped into *Jurassic World*.'

'But you can't go around shooting at them with a bow and arrow, either,' Mia said. 'Someone is going to get seriously injured. Is that what you want, Grandmère?'

'It depends on who it is that I've injured.' Grandmère looked thoughtful.

'I have an idea,' I said, before Mia could get even more upset. 'Why don't I stay here and help Grandmère with the iguanas? That's a much better idea than my going to royal school. I've learned so much more from being around both of you than I ever could in school, anyway. See, I can prove it . . . I've been writing down everything you've taught me.'

I opened my notebook and read aloud so that they'd know I'd been paying attention:

○ Royals never chew gum in public because that makes them look like a cow chewing cud.

- Royals do not allow their poodle puppies to dig (or bury things they've dragged from the kitchen) in the exotic flower beds of the Royal Genovian Gardens, especially considering how few there are left, thanks to the iguanas.

- Royals do not drop things from the top of the Grand Royal Staircase on the fourth floor all the way down to the grand entranceway in the Great Hall as 'an experiment' to see whether they will bounce, as the grand entranceway is made of very expensive Carrara marble.

- Royals do not put seven lumps of sugar into their tea. Three is more than adequate.

- Royals never spit food back on to their plates because they don't like it. They swallow what's in their mouths, then lay down their forks and sit quietly. When asked why they aren't eating, instead of saying they dislike the food (since this is an insult to the chef), they should say that they are 'leaving room for the next course', which they've heard is going to be even more delicious. If they dislike that course as well, they should repeat the advice above until the end of the meal, at which point they should politely thank their host and go home to eat a sandwich.
- Royals do not slide down the Hall of Portraits in their socks during public touring hours.
- Royals send thank-you notes promptly, and in their own handwriting.
- Royals may apply lip gloss at the table, and even sparkle lip balm, but a royal may not 'fix her braids' at the table, even a braid that is 'bothering her'. She must instead retire to the bathroom to do so.

- Royals act confident at all times, even when they least feel it.

Mia smiled at me kindly. 'That's very nice, Olivia. And I understand that you feel insecure about starting a new school. But I'm confident that you'll love it at the RGA — and learn much more there than you could staying here. In addition to all the regular academic courses, they have art and fencing and self-defence and drama classes — even horseback-riding lessons. It's not just dance and deportment any more, like it used to be.'

'Ah,' Grandmère said, a faraway look in her eye, 'dance and deportment. How well I remember my days at the RGA! My waltzing partner was Prince Wilhelm of Prussia. Such a good-looking boy — unfortunate about his lack of coordination, though. It took months before the feeling came back in my toes.'

Mia frowned at Grandmère. 'That isn't going to happen to Olivia. The RGA is different now. It offers state-of-the-art education for modern young royals. So, Olivia, for a variety of reasons — but mostly because I'll feel much, much more comfortable about your safety this week if I know you're there — I'm afraid you're going to have to add one more thing to your list: Royals go to school, because they understand that education is the key to success in life.'

I couldn't believe it, but I didn't want to seem uncooperative. After all, she's the bride, and I'm only a junior bridesmaid. Junior bridesmaids are too old to be flower girls, but not old enough yet to be full-fledged bridesmaids . . . though really the only thing bridesmaids can do that junior bridesmaids can't is drive.

'And,' my sister added, 'it's only for a week. School gets out for the year on Friday.'

That's when I said, 'All right.' It seemed the gracious thing to do, especially since what bridesmaids are really supposed to do is *emotionally* support the bride, even if what the bride wants is completely and totally *dumb*.

I think Mia must have noticed that's what I was thinking, since she said, 'I promise it won't be so bad, Olivia. And you won't be alone. Rocky will be going to the RGA, too. Madame Alain sent a letter about him, as well.'

If this was supposed to make me feel better, it didn't.

Technically, Rocky and I have a lot in common, so you'd think we'd get along great.

- Princess Mia is his big sister, too.
- He just had to move to Genovia.
- His dad died, just like my mom died (well, not in the exact same way, but we're both half-orphans).
- His mom, Helen Thermopolis, and my dad are getting married some day (after the foundation gets fixed).

But we have a lot more *not* in common:

- He's not in line for the throne, so he never has to go to high tea or state dinners.
- He's nine, and sometimes he *really* acts like it, if you know what I mean.

- He loves the iguanas and spends hours every day trying to think up ways to catch them (but so far never has, because iguanas can be very quick when they want to be).
- All he ever talks about is dinosaurs, farting and space travel. In that order.

Even worse, he's going to be the ring bearer in Mia's wedding. The ring bearer, unlike a junior bridesmaid, has only one job to do, and that's walk down the aisle carrying the wedding rings.

All I can say to that is, if those rings actually make it all the way down the aisle and on to Princess Mia's and Michael's fingers, it will be a miracle.

Whose idea was it to slide down the Hall of Portraits in our socks? Rocky's.

Whose idea was it to do the 'experiment' and drop all those things from the fourth floor? Rocky's.

But did Rocky get in trouble for doing those things? No, because I was there, too, and I took the blame.

I know I should have been the mature one who said, 'No. Stop. Let's not do these things. They're disrespectful and wrong.'

But doing them was a *tiny* bit fun (and also Grandmère loves Rocky almost as much as she loves me, and she thinks his 'boyish high jinks' are hilarious).

Still, finding out that Rocky's going to the same school as me? Not making anything better, since it means I'm probably only going to get in more trouble.

Then, though I didn't think it could be possible, things got even worse!

'Oh, and your cousin Luisa,' Mia added cheerfully. 'She goes to the RGA, as well, Olivia. You met her at the bridesmaid gown fitting last month, remember?'

Remember? How could I forget? Especially since my cousin — three or four times removed — Lady

Luisa Ferrari is my same age but looks, talks and acts like she's in high school, practically.

I suppose that's because Lady Luisa is from the Italian side of the family. Italians are very sophisticated. Instead of saying hello or goodbye, they say *ciao*.

Of course I only found out that *ciao* is pronounced 'chow', and not 'kee-yow', like it's spelled in books, *after* I said it wrong in front of Luisa.

I don't think it was very polite of Luisa to laugh so hard at my mistake. You're supposed to try to make newcomers to your country feel welcome, not make fun of them, even when they say or do dumb things because they're not familiar with your language or culture. That's one of the many things I've learned during my princess lessons (but actually I already knew it, because I'm not rude enough to laugh at other people's mistakes, unlike *some* people I could mention).

'You two looked as if you were getting along

really well at the fitting, from the way you were laughing,' Mia went on.

'Ha,' I said faintly. 'Sure, yeah, we were.'

How could Mia not have seen that Luisa was the only one laughing? And that she was laughing at *me*?

And that after Luisa got done laughing at me for mispronouncing *ciao* (which wasn't my fault), all she'd done the whole rest of the dress fitting was talk non-stop about *another* one of our distant cousins, Khalil, who is going to be a groomsman.

Groomsmen are like bridesmaids, only boys. During the wedding, Michael is going to be crowned Mia's prince consort, so he needs to have as many groomsmen as she has bridesmaids, so it looks as grand as possible. But apparently Michael doesn't have that many male relatives, so Mia is letting him borrow some of ours.

Of course, Khalil is the prince of some country I have never heard of. I think it doesn't even exist any more, due to one of the wars that's causing all the refugees to flee to safety here in Genovia. That's why he's a boarding-school student at the RGA, and why his parents now live in Paris, France.

I swear, I went from having practically no family to having more cousins (all three and four times removed, so it's like we're not even really related, but still) than I can count!

And all of them are royalty of some kind.

'Prince Khalil is the cutest boy in the RGA.' Luisa had gone on and on. 'He is also the tallest, with the thickest, curliest brown hair you've ever seen. So we will make the best pair when we dance at the ball after the royal wedding.'

'Oh, Prince *Khalil*,' another one of my cousins, Marguerite, had said knowingly. (Marguerite preferred to be called Meg, but Grandmère says nicknames aren't allowed when you're royalty.) She pronounced it Kuh-*leel*, with the emphasis on the *leel*. 'He's cute.'

'But he wants to be a herpetologist,' said another cousin, Victorine. 'That's not cute.'

'Ugh, yes!' Luisa replied, shuddering. 'But I will soon cure him of *that*.'

I don't know what a herpetologist is, but I agree it doesn't sound very cute. Still, the fact that Luisa wants to cure him of it makes me feel a bit sorry for Prince Khalil.

'Oh yes,' Marguerite said. 'My mother says that once a boy is in love with you, you can make him do anything you want.'

'Yes,' Luisa agreed. 'So as soon as Prince Khalil and I are going out, I will make him do whatever I say, including give up herpetology, then dance *every* dance with me at the wedding reception ball, under the moonlight by the fountain in the Royal Genovian Gardens. It will be so romantic!'

I had to try really hard not to gag out loud at that. None of what Luisa was describing sounded romantic to me . . . especially the part about dancing with a boy by the fountain in the Royal Genovian Gardens!

Of course, Luisa doesn't know how many iguanas there are back here. One of them is bound to fall out of the palm trees on to their heads.

I only hope I'm there to see it when this happens.

'Luisa Ferrari thinks far too highly of herself,' Grandmère said now, stuffing a tea cake into her mouth. 'Just like her grandmother. Did you know that her grandmother, the Baroness Bianca Ferrari, had the nerve to suggest to me that *Luisa* be the one to carry your bridal train in the wedding, Mia? She said she thinks Olivia doesn't have enough experience yet as a royal to do it, and might embarrass the family on international television.'

What? I almost choked on a tea cake of my own at hearing this. How hard is it to carry *a bridal train*? It's only a dress, for goodness' sake.

Also, I've had lots of experience in front of the camera! I've been doing the Smile and Wave for weeks.

'Grandmère,' Mia said in a warning voice, possibly because she'd noticed my expression once again.

'Of course,' Grandmère went on, 'Luisa probably *would* have carried your train if we hadn't found Olivia. The fact that Luisa still gets to be a junior bridesmaid ought to be enough for her grandmother. Did you know that woman had the nerve to ask me for *ten* extra tickets to your reception, Amelia? How we're ever going to fit all the people *we've* invited, I don't know, let alone the riffraff Bianca Ferrari thinks she can—'

'Grandmère!' Mia must have noticed that I looked a little freaked out, since she asked, 'Are you all right, Olivia? You're not worried about starting this new school, are you?'

Uh, yes! And I could think of a million reasons — not even counting Luisa! — that I should be.

At my last school back in New Jersey, a girl had really, really disliked me, for no better reason than that I'd been born.

Well, born a princess. But still!

And now they want me to go to a school that's filled with girls (and boys) who've been royal their whole lives, and have had years of training at it, while I've only been at it for a few weeks?

I'm a pretty confident person, as Nishi would agree. She says I'm an optimist (not only because I'm a Sagittarius but because we took a quiz online at her house once that confirmed it). I really don't let things get me down for long.

But it's kind of hard to feel optimistic about this new school — especially knowing that Lady Luisa is going to be there, too. In fact, I think I could turn out to be an even worse disaster there than I was at my old school! People like me, who enjoy drawing better than sports or playing video games or fashion or dancing, are usually never that popular anyway.

And princesses who've only just found out they're princesses and who also like to draw?

Well, I'm not sure, but there's a chance I could be the first person in my family to flunk out of the Royal Genovian Academy.

But all I said in answer to Mia's question was, 'No. I'm sure everything is going to be great!'

Because there's one last thing royals are supposed to do:

∘ Project a positive attitude.

Even though positive is not what I'm feeling right now, about school, this wedding, or much of anything, really.

Sunday 14 June
11.00 p.m.
My Room
Genovian Palace

Tomorrow is my first day at the Royal Genovian Academy — or, as Nishi *still* keeps calling it, 'princess school' — and I can't sleep.

And it's not because Nishi keeps texting me, wanting to know:

- What I'm going to wear (no choice: there's a uniform)
- How I'm going to do my hair (headband)
- Whether or not she's going to need to bring a hair dryer (no: all the bedrooms in the palace

have their own en-suite bathrooms, which means each has a hairdryer and of course mini soaps and bottles of shampoo and conditioner made from the essence of real Genovian orange blossom)

Because after answering her zillionth question, I finally turned my phone off.

(I HAVE to make her understand about the time difference. Genovia is six hours ahead of the United States. But I don't think she's ever going to grasp that fact until she gets here.)

At dinner Grandmère was like, 'Don't forget, Olivia, tonight you're really going to need your beauty sleep. Every woman should sleep at least eight hours a night so that she can wake refreshed upon the morning to battle the new day!'

But I can't get *any* kind of sleep, beauty or even regular.

Which is ridiculous because I'm lying in a canopy bed shaped like a boat under a ceiling painted to look like the night sky, with Snowball cuddled up to me.

And sitting on the nightstand next to me is a tray that had warm milk and cookies on it that the royal kitchen sent up to help me doze off. I ate every single one!

So why can't I sleep?

Maybe it's what my dad said when he came in to wish me goodnight and I asked him — quietly, so Grandmère and Mia wouldn't overhear — if he thought I was going to make any friends in school tomorrow.

'Of course!' he said, looking surprised. 'Your problem isn't going to be not making *any* friends, Olivia, but making *too many* friends. You're going to make so many friends, we're not going to be able to fit them all here in the palace!'

I laughed because this was a joke, of course. The maximum capacity for the ballroom is five hundred (I know because there's a tiny gold sign on the wall that says so, as required by Genovian fire code, and also because that's how many are invited to the wedding).

But it was also a joke because only 120 students go to the Royal Genovian Academy (from kindergarten through to twelfth grade). Also because no one could *possibly* have five hundred friends in real life . . .

Unless, of course, she's a princess. This was something Mia had warned me about at dinner.

'Just to let you know . . . it's possible that at this new school *some* people might only want to become your friend so they can use you for your celebrity status,' she'd said over the very delicious 'back to school' dinner that the kitchen staff had thoughtfully prepared for me (with all my favourite things): mini-burgers, skinny fries, coconut shrimp, mac and cheese, with ice-cream sundaes for dessert.

(Grandmère asked Chef Bernard for his resignation letter when she saw all this, because, she said, there wasn't a single green thing on the table. But then he brought her a salade niçoise, so she forgave him.)

'Just be careful that the people you hang out with like you for *you*, and not because you're a princess who might get them a ton of likes on their social media pages, or last-minute invitations to my wedding, or something,' Mia said.

I must have looked alarmed, since she'd quickly added, 'Not that this is going to happen to you! It's just . . . well, it might have happened to me once.'

It's possible that this piece of advice is contributing to my inability to sleep.

Even Grandmère wasn't as comforting as she usually is when she came in to say goodnight.

'I've ordered the bulletproof car to take you to school tomorrow, Olivia. It will be ready for you at eight o'clock. Don't be late, as after it drops you off, I'll need it to return to the palace to take me to a sporting goods shop in Cap-d'Ail. They supposedly stock an air rifle that's superb for pest control.'

I sat straight up in bed. Carlos! 'Grandmère, no! *Please* don't shoot any of the iguanas. I'm sure we can think of some other way to get rid of them.'

'Shoot the iguanas?' She looked at her reflection in the gold-framed mirror above my dressing table and straightened her tiara. 'I haven't the slightest idea what you mean. I only mean to frighten them into going to someone else's garden . . . Bianca Ferrari's, perhaps. If there's anyone who deserves iguanas in her pool, it's her.'

'Grandmère, *don't*. And why can't I walk to school? The RGA is right around the corner from the palace.'

'A princess, walk to school?' Grandmère sniffed. 'Certainly not. You'll ride in the bulletproof Mercedes with your bodyguard, Serena.'

'Why?' I asked curiously.

'Once you become a well-known public figure, there'll always be someone out there looking to kidnap you. It's wiser not to make it easier for them by giving them the opportunity.'

My sister (who happened to be walking down the hall at that very moment) gasped and said, 'Grandmère, really? You're going to frighten her.'

'I'm not frightened,' I said. 'Serena has been giving me self-defense lessons.'

'Nevertheless.' Mia looked stern. 'This is an unsuitable topic of discussion for bedtime.'

'Pfuit,' Grandmère said. 'No one has been kidnapped in Genovia in years — which is unfortunate because I can think of quite a few people I'd like to get rid of, especially this week. Bianca Ferrari comes to mind.'

Mia frowned. 'Say good*night* to Olivia, Grandmère.'

'Goodnight, Olivia,' Grandmère said, and went to her own room, probably to look up more ways to get rid of iguanas.

It's hard to sleep when you're starting a new school in the morning . . . especially one where everyone is royal.

But I guess I have no choice but to believe my dad that I'm going to make so many friends, we're not even going to be able to fit them all in the palace. Why shouldn't I? He's never lied to me before . . .

Well, except for neglecting to tell me for my whole life up until recently that he's the prince of a foreign country.

But that wasn't a lie, exactly, because my mom asked him not to tell me, for my own safety. And that turned out OK in the end.

So far, anyway.

Monday 15 June
11.25 a.m.
Royal Genovian Academy

OK, I'm having a hard time projecting a positive attitude. Things are not going well at the new school.

And I've only been here for three hours!

But I'm not going to text my bodyguard, Serena, to come and get me (she's playing cards outside in the courtyard with all the rest of the drivers and bodyguards), because then the paparazzi will only make fun of me for being a quitter.

I could tell things at this school were going to go badly right away when Mia and I walked in and

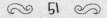

there was Madame Alain — the head of the school — standing in front of her office waiting for us . . .

. . . with my cousin Lady Luisa!

Of course Lady Luisa looked *amazing* in her school uniform — which is at least better than the uniform I used to have to wear at my old school, because it's blue and white, not plaid and white, and the girls have the option to wear shorts if they want (which I do, because who wouldn't want to, in a school that's across the street from a beach?).

But it's still a uniform, and so not exactly stylish.

But who looks stylish in it, anyway?

My cousin Lady Luisa, that's who!

Although of course she'd chosen to wear the skirt instead of shorts. But she'd had the skirt hemmed as short as it could possibly be and still meet the minimum dress-code requirement.

'Welcome, Princess Olivia,' Madame Alain said, after the band got done playing the Genovian national anthem.

That's right. The entire school band was there to

greet me! It burst into the Genovian national anthem the minute we walked in.

This was totally embarrassing, even though it happens pretty much everywhere I go now.

But I didn't expect it at my new *school*.

'We're so delighted to have you here at last.'

Somehow Madame Alain said the words *at last* like I'd just been lounging around the palace pool for the past few weeks, doing nothing, which isn't at all true!

I was lounging around there reading books from the palace library with my sister.

And when I wasn't doing that, I was doing work of national importance, such as visiting sick children in the Genovian hospital and helping to pick out floral arrangements for the tables at the prenuptial and reception banquets. It's very hard to find purple flowers that won't look too small on a table for fifty (of which there are going to be at least ten, so far).

But I said thanks, because that's what princesses are supposed to do.

Madame Alain curtsied and said, 'The Royal Genovian Academy is so honoured to receive you. As you can see, here we train young royals from all over the world.' She raised a hand to show me all the portraits on the wall of the royals who'd graduated from the RGA, each wearing a crown and a smile on their face. 'All of them can represent their sovereign nation with pride because of the excellent education they received here. Some of our students come from nations so far away that they must board with us, while others, like yourself, Princess, have family nearby, and so are day students.'

'Oh,' I said, staring at all the portraits. Some were so faded by all the bright Genovian sunlight pouring in through the windows that you could barely make out if they were men or women. That's how old they were. 'Neat.'

'Madame Alain,' Mia said, in a kind-of-fake voice. She looked about as thrilled to be there as I was. I think she knew Madame Alain from somewhere, but I don't know where. 'Thank you so much for accepting Olivia so late into the term. I'm sure she'll make you very proud, as she has all of us.'

Oh no! This was way too much pressure. I could see Luisa staring down at me from under her eyelids with a tiny superior smile on her face. I couldn't believe that if I had to have a relative my own age in this school, it had to be *her*, with her long legs and long nails and long, silky blond hair.

'I'm sure Princess Olivia will do marvellously here at the RGA,' Madame Alain went on with a wide smile. 'And to make sure, we've selected one of our best and most popular day students, Lady Luisa Ferrari, to be her royal guide for the next few days.

Luisa's been attending the RGA since kindergarten, so she knows everything there is to know about our training academy for modern royals.'

'I really do,' Luisa said with a curtsy to my sister.

'Oh,' Mia said. 'That's so sweet of you, Luisa.'

Ugh. Ugh ugh ugh ugh ugh ugh ugh ugh.

'Wonderful,' Madame Alain said, beaming. 'I can see that these girls are going to be best friends already.'

I know this isn't a very princess-y thing to write or even think, but Madame Alain must be blind. 'Uh,' Mia said, looking around, because even though the walls of the school are pretty thick — almost every building in Genovia is made of three-foot-wide stone, since the village was built in medieval times with the goal of keeping out marauding invaders — you could hear someone screaming from somewhere in the lower-form building. I couldn't believe it. *Rocky*. 'I think I'll just leave Olivia in your very competent hands, then, Madame, and go and . . .' Her voice trailed off.

'Er,' Madame Alain said. The screaming was getting louder.

'Yes. Perhaps I'd better go with you . . .'

Perhaps? With that kind of noise, *perhaps* they'd better call the fire department, the police department, and the entire Genovian army.

Rocky had already had one major meltdown at breakfast — insisting he wouldn't wear the school uniform, because 'future paleontologist-astronauts' like him shouldn't have to dress like everyone else (which makes no sense, because astronauts wear uniforms. They're called space suits).

He'd even thrown his shoes at Michael (who made me laugh when he expertly caught them and threw them back, even though Mia said he shouldn't have done this, because future princes aren't supposed to throw shoes at their brothers-in-law at breakfast).

But I think Rocky deserved it. I feel like nine-year-olds (even ones who are trying to adjust to living in a palace in a new country) should know better than to throw their shoes at people. Even worse, Rocky's poor mom, Helen, and my dad had to drag him screaming and kicking (with his shoes off) to school in one car while Mia took me to school in the bulletproof one that Grandmère was so anxious to have back so she could go shopping later.

Although this ended up being fine with me because even though I've never had a parent take me to school before, I definitely didn't want my dad, *the retired prince of the country*, taking me to school on my first day. Talk about embarrassing!

And even though I'd never say this in front of Dad — because I wouldn't want to hurt his feelings — everyone likes Princess Mia better than him anyway. I think it's because Mia wears better clothes. Dad wears boring old suits and ties. Mia always wears pretty dresses with high heels and hats, and of course her big engagement ring that Michael gave her, which is a genuine ENGINEERED diamond, so it's conflict-free and environmentally friendly.

But Rocky having a meltdown that you could hear all the way from a different building at school wasn't even the *worst thing* that's happened yet.

As soon as Mia and Madame Alain hurried away to go and see if they could help Dad and Helen with Rocky, Luisa turned to me and went, 'Kee-yow, Olivia.'

Kee-yow! Kee-yow instead of *ciao*!

This made me so mad — even though she had one of her tiny Luisa Ferrari smiles on her face to show she was only kidding or whatever — I thought I was going to burst.

'Look, Luisa,' I said. 'I told you before, I made a mistake mispronouncing that word. Everyone makes mistakes. The polite thing to do is forget it and move on. So can we please just do that?'

'I will never forget it,' Luisa said in her Italian accent, still smiling and now swishing around some of her long blond hair. 'Because it was the most adorable thing I ever saw. *You* are the most adorable thing I ever saw. Does everyone in America wear their hair like that?'

Then she did the rudest thing. She grabbed a handful of my hair! Right in the middle of the hallway of my new school, in front of the band, who were still packing up their instruments!

'Hey!' I yelled, yanking my head away from her. 'What are you doing? Cut it out!'

'What is wrong?' Luisa asked, her eyes all wide and innocent. 'I only wanted to touch your hair. I've never felt anything like it. Why are you offended?'

'Because it's rude to go around touching other people's hair.' Was this girl crazy? 'How would you like it if I did that to you?'

I reached out, grabbed a handful of Luisa's long, silky golden hair, then tugged it.

'Aiii!' she cried, wrenching her golden locks away from me. 'What are you doing? My maid Fabriana spent a half-hour straightening my hair this morning!'

'See? Now you know what it feels like.'

Meanwhile, all the people in the band — some of whom were older boys and girls, possibly in high school — were staring at us. Some were even laughing. Talk about embarrassing!

'Kee-yow, Olivia,' Luisa said, pulling out her mobile to check her hair in the camera, making sure it was still perfectly straight. 'You are crazy. We are cousins. Cousins can touch each other's hair.'

'Not without asking first,' I said. 'It's disrespectful. And stop saying "kee-yow"!'

Luisa snorted and put her phone away. 'Fine, I will not touch your hair again, Your Very Royal Highness. Now, we had better get going. Even though you are the princess of Genovia, I am sure Monsieur Montclair will still be angry with us for being late. I am the best dancer in the class, so they need me before they can start, because everyone follows my every move.'

I had no idea what she was talking about — THEN.

But I do NOW.

Because guess what? Everything Mia said about how they have fencing and art and self-defence and horseback-riding classes here?

Well, she was right.

But not when there's going to be *a royal wedding in one week.*

Because when there's going to be a royal wedding in one week, everyone in the entire country goes COMPLETELY BANANAS. All anyone can talk about is the pretty princess bride (Mia) and her handsome prince-consort-to-be (Michael), and how there's going to be a national holiday to celebrate the wedding, so everyone is going to get a three-day weekend, and how, on the day of the ceremony itself, there's going to be:

- A parade
- Fireworks
- Free champagne for adults
- Free ice cream for everyone
- A military salute (during which the cannons on top of the palace walls will be shot off)
- Free carriage rides through the village square
- A lit-up boat parade through the marina at night

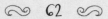

- A ball
- Commemorative stamps featuring both my sister's *and* Michael's heads

But that's not why all normal classes at the Royal Genovian Academy are suspended! No, all normal classes are suspended so the 120 students of the RGA can concentrate on rehearsing 'All Roads Lead to Genovia', the most famous traditional folk song of Genovia, which *we're going to perform in front of Princess Mia and her future prince consort, Michael, when they stop by to visit the school on Friday, the day before their wedding!*

As if that isn't bad enough, we're going to be singing it while wearing the traditional national costume of Genovia, which for girls involves something called a dirndl, which is a dress with a stiff puffy skirt and a tight black corset!

But for boys the national costume of Genovia is even worse: It's lederhosen, which is a kind of overalls, only with shorts!

No wonder poor Rocky was screaming so loudly.

Madame Alain — who'd rushed back to the sixth-grade room after getting Rocky 'settled' — said, apparently not noticing my horror, 'Our performance of "All Roads Lead to Genovia" will be the Royal Genovian Academy's wedding gift to your sister and the future Prince Michael! We've been rehearsing it for over a week now. But of course you mustn't tell her! It's to be a surprise.'

Oh, Mia is going to be surprised, all right.

'Your joining us, Your Highness,' Madame Alain went on, 'will truly be the icing on the cake!'

Icing on the cake? More like the crumbly bits of gravel at the bottom of a mud pie!

I know it isn't polite or princessy to correct your elders, so I couldn't exactly go, 'Uh, Madame Alain, I'm sorry, but there is no possible way that my sister and Michael are going to stop by your school on Friday, the day before their wedding, to watch us perform some goofy song in even goofier costumes, because I've seen their schedule, and they're going to be way too busy. For one thing, that's the day they're having their final wedding rehearsal — at which I have to be, by the way, and so does Luisa and Rocky, because we're *in the wedding*! It's also when all of the out-of-town guests who aren't here already are going to start arriving, such as the president of the United States, the king and queen of Bhutan, and the *queen of England*, just to name a few! That's also the day of the prenuptial dinner, which we have to get ready for and attend, and of course when Grandmère and I have to do all the final checks on the gowns, the flowers, the food, and the seating arrangements, *and* when Mia and Michael have to pack for their honeymoon in the Greek isles, which they're going to on the royal yacht! So, even though it's a really nice thought and all, and I'm sure my sister would be extremely grateful, it's never, ever going to happen.'

Except that Madame Alain — and all the students in the class — looked so happy and excited, I couldn't say a word about any of that. I didn't want to disappoint them.

So I only smiled and went, 'Oh. That is so nice. But, er, perhaps you might want to check with the palace about my sister's schedule—'

'Oh, I already have!' Madame Alain said. 'I consulted with Prince Phillipe himself. And his office informed me that it's all arranged!'

Prince Phillipe? My *dad*?

My dad is very amazing and wonderful in many ways, but he is not exactly organized, or even aware of anything that's been going on, other than his work on the summer palace and listening to Mia and Rocky's mom, Helen, talk about how much she hates her cream-coloured mother-of-the-bride dress (which I personally think could really be improved with a little purple dye).

The father of the bride's only duties, according to Grandmère, are to:

- Show up to walk the bride down the aisle
- Make a nice speech during the reception
- Do the father/daughter dance
- Pay for everything
- Loan the mother of the bride his handkerchief if she starts to cry

So I'm pretty sure my dad has NO IDEA his office

agreed to schedule a visit from my sister and her future husband to the RGA on the day before their wedding.

But all I said was 'Oh. Great,' with a huge fake smile on my face.

Madame Alain looked really pleased and said, 'I'm so glad you think so, Your Highness! Now please take your seat. We've arranged a very special new desk for you!'

I went to the 'very special new desk' they'd arranged for me — all decorated with my name, Her Royal Highness Olivia, in sparkly stars — only to see they'd wedged it right between Luisa's desk and . . .

Luisa's crush, Prince Khalil.

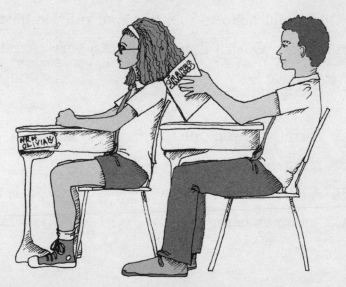

Luisa looked pretty unhappy about this. She flounced down into her seat, then whipped out her mobile and began furiously texting.

I don't know who she was texting (her mom, maybe, to complain?), but it

didn't seem to be Prince Khalil. He wasn't on his phone. He was reading a book about snakes.

I know that as a wildlife illustrator I should appreciate all animals. But snakes? I feel the same about snakes as I do about iguanas (with the exception of Carlos): No, thank you.

Khalil said hello to me, but that's it. He hasn't even smiled, which I don't think is a very friendly way to behave for:

A. A cousin, even one three or four times removed

B. A prince

C. A human being

Maybe he's afraid if he says anything else to me, Luisa will get even more mad? I guess I'd be scared of Luisa, too, if I were Khalil. Although he probably doesn't know what she has planned for him on Saturday, with the dancing and the fountain and the moonlight.

Even worse, my other cousins three or four times removed, Marguerite and Victorine, are also in this class (and also wearing skirts, like Luisa, not shorts. I'm the ONLY girl in this class who chose the shorts instead of the skirt)! They keep looking over at me and whispering and laughing to each other.

Great.

Now Madame Pinchot, the singing instructor, is making us stand up to practise.

(Oops, wait, not me. She's upset that I don't know the words to 'All Roads Lead to Genovia', which is apparently *the* most famous song in the entire country, except for the national anthem.)

I want to raise my hand and go, 'Uh, no offense, but I only just got here a month ago. Also, I'm pretty sure my sister's future husband doesn't know it, either, and I think as a wedding gift he would rather have a *Star Wars* calendar or socks or really anything *Star Wars*, because he really likes *Star Wars*.'

But I know that would be rude.

Also, I don't know what my sister would like as a wedding present (besides donations to her favourite charities) because she basically has everything. Probably she would like a candy bar, because she told me the other day that the twins are making her hungry all the time, especially for chocolate, but she's afraid that if she eats too much of it, she's going to explode out of her wedding gown, and then Sebastiano, the famous fashion designer who made her wedding dress and all our bridesmaid gowns, will have a fit. He's also a cousin of ours from the Italian side of the family, and though he's very, very talented, he's also very, very dramatic.

I apologized to Madame Pinchot for not knowing the words to 'All Roads Lead to Genovia' and said, 'I'll try to learn them as soon as possible, Madame.'

She's given me a paper with the words on it and told me to memorize them. They don't seem that hard, but they don't make much sense, either:

'All Roads Lead to Genovia'
(Author Unknown)

I've travelled far
So far have I roamed
But Genovia
Will always be home

Land of green palms
And ocean so blue
No other land
Can compare to you

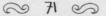

No matter how far
I happen to roam
To Genovia
I'll always come home

Genovia, Genovia
Land of green and blue
Genovia, Genovia
All roads lead to you

(Repeat seven times)

But we have to sing it in traditional medieval Genovian, which is a mix of Italian and French.

So basically it sounds like an old man gargling with onion soup.

Oh well. This is the least I can do for my new country.

I guess things can't get worse.

Monday 15 June
1.35 p.m.
Royal Genovian Academy

Things have got worse. Much, much worse!

Now I not only have to learn a stupid song (I'm sorry, I know I shouldn't call one of the oldest, most traditional songs of the country over which I could some day rule stupid, but it is), but I also have to dance with a stupid PRINCE!

I don't mean to make it sound like I'm prejudiced against princes, because I'm not. I know some princes who are very nice. My dad is a prince, and he's great (when he's not yelling about how long it's going to take to fix the foundation over at the summer palace or how much this wedding is costing).

Michael isn't a prince yet, but I think he's going to make a fine one when he's crowned (at the wedding), even if he's going to be only a prince consort.

Consorts are the spouse of the ruler of the country and aren't actually in line to inherit the throne. Consorts don't have to come to high tea, or help make decisions of state, or even wear their crowns. They just have to look good in photos and say things like 'Everything is going to be all right' to the ruler.

But the prince I got assigned to dance with today? He's a real prince, and he is totally *not nice*! He's barely even OK!

And I know we're not supposed to judge other people, at least not until we've walked a mile in their shoes.

But Prince Gunther is the WORST!!!!

I know why he was the only person left in class without a dance partner, and that's because he's a boarding student who:

- Wears shower shoes to school with kneesocks and shorts
- Picks his nose, then flicks what he finds in there at Monsieur Montclair when he isn't looking, and then laughs
- Makes fart noises out of his mouth every chance he gets
- Likes to show off his 'guns', which are what he calls his arm muscles
- Has green hair — not because he dyed it green, which would be cool, but because it turned green from all the swimming he does in the school pool
- Brags that he's such a good swimmer, he's going to be in the next Olympics

But I don't see how this is possible. Surely his native land of Austria wouldn't want a green-haired bogey flinger representing the country in the Olympics, even if he *is* a prince.

Because of all the swimming, Gunther really does have huge shoulders and biceps. So when I have

to take his arm in the part of the dance where 'the Genovian gentleman promenades his Genovian lady' down the centre, Prince Gunther flexes his biceps under my fingers.

This is not only gross, it practically cuts off my circulation, because Prince Gunther squeezes my hand so tightly against his side.

I want to complain about this to Mademoiselle Justine, the dance instructor, but I'm not sure if Prince Gunther is doing it on purpose to show off or if this is just how boys' arms work. I'm not very experienced with boys other than Rocky, and he's only nine, so how would I know?

The last time it happened, I got so grossed out that I ran away from Prince Gunther and joined the girls on their side of the room. After each rehearsal, the boys and girls split off to opposite sides of the room. I don't know why. We just do.

'Kee-yow, Olivia,' Luisa said when she saw my face. 'What's wrong?'

I didn't even get mad at her this time for saying 'kee-yow', because I was so freaked out by what had just happened. At a moment like that, even the companionship of someone like Luisa was welcome.

'Every time we promenade,' I whispered, 'Prince Gunther flexes like this.' I showed her.

'Ewwwwwwww!' Luisa cried. 'He is so disgusting!'

Of course all the other girls overheard and then gathered around, wanting to know what we were talking about. Even the shy girl — the only other princess in class besides me, Komiko, who never speaks to anyone at all, as far as I can tell.

I should have known that Luisa can't keep a secret. Now every single girl in our entire class refers to Prince Gunther as 'the Flexer', which I feel bad about. I'm the princess of Genovia. I'm supposed to be setting a good example, not spreading gossip about other people.

'Maybe he's not doing it on purpose,' I said.

'No, he is definitely doing it on purpose,' Luisa said. She considers herself an expert on boys. 'He isn't like Prince Khalil. Prince Khalil would never do something like that. He is a perfect gentleman . . . except, of course, that he will *not stop* reading about snakes.'

She said this last part while gritting her teeth and staring across the room. It's true! In between dance rehearsals, Prince Khalil heads to his desk to pick up his book about snakes and then reads it.

I haven't seen him speak to Luisa once — except to apologize for stepping on her toes, because of course Prince Khalil is Luisa's dance partner — which must be frustrating for her, since he's her boyfriend-to-be.

'Ah well,' Luisa said, tossing back some of her long hair. 'He wouldn't dare bring that book to the wedding.'

'Of course not,' Marguerite said sympathetically, and patted her on the shoulder. 'Although he could download it to his mobile.'

Luisa looked dismayed. 'He wouldn't!'

'You never know,' Victorine said. 'The Flexer would do something like that. He sits next to me, and all day long he draws mean pictures of Madame Alain, giving her a very big . . .' She pointed to her butt. 'You know what.'

I was shocked. The rest of the girls giggled, even Komiko, who is so shy she hardly ever even smiles.

'Maybe he's just a bad drawer,' I suggested. 'I like to draw, too, but sometimes it's hard to get everything to look right. Maybe the Flexer isn't very good at drawing, so it just *looks* like he's sketching Madame Alain with a very big . . . you know what.'

'Kee-yow, Olivia,' Luisa said with a smirk. 'You are so immature! Of course he is drawing her that way on purpose. All the boys in this class are so babyish. Well, except for my Prince Khalil. He is perfect.'

I've only been here a few hours and I'm already

getting very tired of hearing about how perfect Prince Khalil is.

'But if that's true about Prince Gunther doing those mean drawings,' I said, 'we should tell someone. That's not very royal behaviour . . . or even very nice.'

'But a royal never tattles.' Princess Komiko actually said something!

I had to think about that one. 'Actually, I think it's probably *more* royal to tattle in some cases than it is not to tattle. Like in cases where someone might be hurt. And it's wrong to make fun of your teachers. That could hurt their feelings.'

Luisa blinked her wide blue eyes. 'But if we tattle on Prince Gunther and he gets kicked out of school, then you won't have a dance partner for the performance, Olivia!'

'I'm OK with that,' I said. 'I can make the sacrifice. I have a lot to do on Friday anyway.'

'No, Luisa's right,' Marguerite said. 'We need you, Your Highness. You *and* your adorable baby brother.'

'Well.' Luisa sniffed. 'I don't know if we *need*

her . . . and if you mean Rocky, Marguerite, he's not even really her brother. He's Princess Mia's *half-brother*, and from her mother's side, not her father's. Technically he shouldn't even be going to this school.'

'Hey,' I said angrily. 'He belongs here just as much as anyone else!'

Luisa narrowed her eyes. 'No, he does not. The Royal Genovian Academy is a training school for *royals*, which Rocky is *not.*'

I couldn't believe how snobby she was being. 'He lives in a palace with a royal family!'

Victorine and Marguerite looked impressed by my argument.

'It's true, Luisa,' said Victorine. 'He does.'

'Oh, right. Of course.' Luisa laughed. 'I was only joking. Don't be so sensitive, Princess Olivia.'

Grandmère told me that it's rude for a royal to say something mean, then tell the other person they're 'sensitive' for getting offended. At least, I'm pretty sure she did.

But before I could tell Luisa this, Mademoiselle

Justine, the dancing instructor, clapped her hands and made us return to our places. 'Ladies, ladies! Less talking, more dancing, please.'

Not five seconds later, Gunther was squeezing my fingers to death again. Not that it even mattered, since I couldn't get any of the steps right. I'm definitely the worst dancer in the whole class. I think Mademoiselle Justine wanted to cry.

'Please,' she said to me. 'Please go home after school today and practise, Your Highness. Your footwork, your arms . . . all of it. Just all of it . . .'

'I will,' I promised.

But all I want to do when I get home is cry. Preferably in a bubble bath.

Monday 15 June
8.15 p.m.
Royal Genovian Bedroom

When I got home from school today, the first thing I did (after scooping up Snowball, who ran to greet me at the side of the limo, and letting her lick me all over my face) was knock on Dad's office door.

'WHO IS IT?' Dad yelled. 'I SAID I WASN'T TO BE DISTURBED!'

Snowball and I went in and found Dad sitting at his huge royal desk, which was covered in blueprints and millions of other papers. He had his reading glasses on top of his bald head, and his feet were

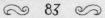

resting on a stuffed boar that my grandfather had shot on a royal hunt way, way before I was born. I call the boar Annabelle because it looks a lot like a girl I used to go to school with who was named Annabelle.

'I don't care how much it's going to cost!' Dad was yelling into his mobile. 'I need it done as soon as possible. As soon as possible, do you understand?' When he saw me, he said in a totally different voice, 'Oh, hello, Olivia sweetheart. How was school today?'

'It was great,' I lied, because I didn't think he needed any more stress. 'Dad, did your office schedule a visit from Mia and Michael to my school this Friday, the *day before the wedding*?'

'I think so. That woman from your school said there was some kind of programme you kids were doing that Mia would want to see. Why, is that a problem?'

'I guess not,' I said, shrugging. 'It might turn out OK. But I think Mia and Michael are probably going to have a lot of other stuff they're going to need to do instead.'

'Like what?' Dad asked, fiddling around with the laptop on his desk.

'Um,' I said. 'I don't know. Greet all the guests. Pack for their honeymoon. Rehearse for the wedding. Stuff like that.'

'Oh, honey,' Dad said. 'We have staff to do all that for them. Well, most of it.'

'Oh,' I said. 'OK. Well, see you at dinner. Good luck with the yelling.'

'Thanks, sweetheart.' He turned back to his phone. 'No, not in two years, two months. I want it done in two months. Do you even know who I am?'

Hmmmm. Probably I should tell Mia — or at least Grandmère — what's going on.

But then I remembered Madame Alain's face when she said the performance was supposed to be a surprise and a wedding gift from the school, and how happy and excited she looked.

I don't want to be the one to spoil it! They've all worked so hard.

And of course Princess Komiko said a royal doesn't tattle (except, as I pointed out, in cases where someone might be hurt).

I can't see how anyone is going to get hurt from this, except maybe my fingers, and they'll probably survive.

So when everyone else asked how school went today, I only said, 'Great!'

Nobody asked for many details because they were too busy dealing with Rocky. *He* may be the one person hurt from all this. I completely forgot about the lederhosen. You could see how a nine-year-old boy from New York City might not want to wear them, even as a surprise wedding gift for his sister.

He hasn't told anyone about them, though. Like me, he's keeping the school's secret. All he said was that he's going to build a rocket ship, powered by his own farts, and fly to the moon and live there with the dinosaurs.

Then he ran up to his room and slammed the door.

'Oh dear,' I overheard Mia say to her mom. 'I don't think Rocky had a very good day at school.'

Of course he didn't! They made him promenade a lady up and down the room all day in his class, too! When he wasn't being forced to sing about how all roads lead to Genovia, land of green and blue.

But instead of saying that, when Mia's mom asked me worriedly if I knew what might be wrong with him, I said, 'Gee, I don't know. Why don't I go check on him?'

'Would you?' She smiled in relief. 'I hate to ask, since I know you've had a long day, too, but Rocky really looks up to you . . .'

This was news to me. Usually Rocky was getting me into trouble.

'Sure,' I said. 'No problem.'

So I did.

Rocky has a room that's almost as nice as mine, but instead of having birds and clouds painted on the walls and ceiling, it has hunting scenes and sailing ships, and his bed doesn't have a canopy.

But he doesn't spend much time in bed, anyway, since he prefers to spend his time in the large cardboard box he's painted to look like a spaceship. That's where I found him.

'Rocky, I know why you're upset,' I said, kneeling beside the box, while Snowball sniffed all around it. 'I think the song is stupid, too. And so is the dance. But we're doing it for Mia and Michael. So at least it's for a good reason.'

'That's easy for you to say.' He pressed some fake buttons he'd painted inside his ship to nowhere. 'You don't have to wear overall shorts!'

'I have it worse. I have to dance with Prince Gunther. He flicks bogeys at the teacher and makes fart noises with his mouth.'

Rocky looked impressed. 'He sounds awesome!'

'Well, he's not. I'd trade Prince Gunther for lederhosen any day.'

'I think we should both run away,' Rocky said. 'Get in. I'm going to the moon.'

I knew Rocky was only pretending about going to the moon. But I got the feeling he wasn't pretending about wanting to run away. Rocky's adjustment to living in Genovia has been a bit like his name: rocky.

Maybe there was something I could do to help make it a tiny bit easier on him.

So I said, 'I'll run away to the moon with you for a little while if you promise that when we come back you'll help me practise dancing, because Mademoiselle Justine says I'm really terrible and I need to work on it. But we can't go to the moon forever, Rocky, because problems aren't something you can run away from. You have to face them, or they'll never get solved.'

He thought about it. 'OK. Get in.'

So Snowball and I got into the fake rocket ship behind him (after I made him promise not to fart on us).

These are the things you sometimes have to do when you're someone's older sibling. When I'm an aunt, I suppose I'll have to be doing things like this all the time. I might even have to do worse things, like change nappies (although Mia says there'll be a nanny. Michael wants to build a robot nanny, but Mia said no).

After we got to the 'moon', I acted like a velociraptor was eating me, so Rocky could 'save' me — even though velociraptors do not really live on the moon, and if they did, and one started eating me, I would have been able to save myself, and Snowball, too.

This seemed to make Rocky feel much better, and by the time we went downstairs to dinner, he told everyone at the table that the Royal Genovian Academy wasn't so bad after all, and he'd go back tomorrow.

Rocky wasn't the only one who seemed to feel better. His mom was so happy that she whispered 'Thank you so much' to me across the twenty-foot dining table, and even from so far away, I could see that she had tears in her eyes.

And Dad was so relieved about the change in Rocky's behaviour, he let us both go outside to play after dinner, instead of making us spend 'family time' with him and all the guests (which, no offense, can get very boring).

Michael said I was a real trooper, and Grandmère said, 'Well, I suppose there's a possibility the RGA might know a thing or two about training royals that I don't — though I doubt it.' Even Mia gave me an extra hug and kiss before I went to bed.

'Olivia, you're the best,' she whispered. 'What on earth did you say to Rocky to get him to want to go to school?'

I shrugged and told her I didn't know. It's OK to lie if the lie doesn't hurt anyone.

'Well, whatever it was, keep it up, please. You've taken one huge worry off my shoulders.'

Maybe that can be my wedding gift to her: taking worries off her shoulders.

It's going to have to be, since I don't have money to buy her anything. I forgot to ask if, as a princess, I get an allowance.

Tuesday 16 June
2.17 a.m.
Royal Genovian Bedroom

< NishiGirl   **OlivGrace >**

How was your first day at princess school???

Nishi, it's 2 in the morning.

Oops, I keep forgetting about the time change! Sorry! Well, how was it?

I told you, it's just regular school! Girls AND boys go there. I sit next to a boy.

< NishiGirl   OlivGrace >

You do? Is he a prince?

Well, yes. But that isn't the point.

What's his name?

Khalil.

Ooooo that's a good name! Did he talk to u?

Not really. Well, he said hello. Nishi, I really have to go to sleep now. My grandmother says you need 8 hours of sleep in order to look and feel your best.

Sorry! But I'm so excited to be coming there! Just 2 more days! So is the prince nice? Will I meet him?

I don't know! He barely talked to me. I guess you'll meet him. He's one of Michael's groomsmen. He's my cousin.

Oh no! So you can't marry him!

Ugh! Why would I want to marry him? But yes, I could marry him if I wanted to, I guess. We're like 3rd cousins 4 times removed or something.

Well, that's a relief! Were there any nice girls?

At school? One, I guess. Komiko. But she barely talked to me, either. She's shy.

Maybe u can help her come out of her shell with ur friendly outgoing personality!

Well, I'll try.

Which Disney prince does Khalil most look like?
Pick one:

- Prince from Snow White
- Prince Charming from Cinderella
- Prince Phillip from Sleeping Beauty
- Prince Eric from The Little Mermaid
- Prince Adam from Beauty and the Beast
- Aladdin

< NishiGirl   OlivGrace >

- Prince Naveen from The Princess and the Frog
- Prince Kristoff from Frozen (because you know he is totally marrying Anna and then he will be a prince consort like your sister's fiancé Michael!)

Nishi, I don't want to disappoint you, but Disney princes aren't real. In real life, princes pick their noses.

OMG!!!!! Prince Khalil picks his nose?

No! Prince Gunther does.

YOU SIT BY TWO PRINCES?????

No. I only sit by one. I dance with the other.

You get to dance with a prince?????

I don't GET to. I HAVE to. He's really gross. And I'm not marrying him, either!!!!

How can he be gross if he's a prince! Isn't he rich?

< NishiGirl   OlivGrace >

Yes, but being rich doesn't make someone cute. You know that! Prince Gunther has green hair and squeezes my fingers super hard when we dance.

But Prince Khalil isn't gross, right? Am I going to get to dance with him? Maybe at the wedding? PLEASE SAY YES!!!!

NISHI! NO! He's my cousin Luisa's crush!!!!

Luisa? The snobby one? Why does SHE get the cute prince? When I get there, we should play a prank on her.

No, we shouldn't! Our job as junior bridesmaids is to HELP my sister, not make things worse by pranking the other junior bridesmaids!!!!

Geesh. OK, I was only kidding. No need to act all princessy about it.

I'm not acting princessy!

U sort of r. U have everything in the world anyone could ever dream of, including a pony and getting to sit next to a cute prince, and now ur acting princessy.

No, I'm not! I'm just saying that not everything is perfect!

Sure, I totally believe u. I have to go now.

Wait, Nishi. I'm sorry. Of course we can prank Luisa if you want to. We can drop an iguana on her head.

Nishi?

Great. Now I can't sleep because Nishi is mad at me.

Well, truthfully, it's also because my sister and all of her friends are out by the pool, laughing and singing, even though every once in a while I hear

Mia say, 'Shush, you guys. People are trying to sleep!'

But then they just laugh even harder.

I also can't sleep because when I went to get a drink of water, I saw that the majordomo — who is basically the head of the entire household staff — had slipped a note under my door informing me that while I was at school today, Snowball stole a piece of ham, a block of butter, and a loaf of fresh-baked bread from the kitchens. One of Chef Bernard's assistants found the bread later on the tennis court. It had little gnaw marks all over it.

The last part of the note said:

Princess Olivia, Chef Bernard would appreciate it if you would kindly control your dog.

Kindest regards,
Henri, Majordomo
Royal Palace
Genovia

Ugh!!!! What am I going to do???

Although I can understand why Snowball gets bored while I'm gone. None of the other dogs at the palace will play with her — Grandmère's dog, Rommel, is too busy following her around, and the rest are all bomb-sniffing dogs doing important work for the Royal Genovian Guard.

And what dog wouldn't get tired of eating dog food? If I had to eat dog food all day, every day, I'd get tired of it, too. Honestly, I think Snowball was trying to make a ham sandwich.

Tuesday 16 June
2.15 p.m.
Royal Genovian Academy

Something good actually happened!

Well . . . something *I* thought was good, at least. I was practising drawing kangaroos at lunch — because kangaroos are still my favourite. I love seeing joeys all snuggled into their pouches — when one of the older students said, 'You know, you're quite good at drawing, Princess Olivia.'

!!!!

I know! I was so surprised. Especially because the girl who said it is a queen!

We don't have kings or queens in Genovia because it's a principality. In principalities, the country is ruled by a prince (or princess). Well, Genovia is actually governed by a prime minister. But the prince (or princess) helps!

Of course, the queen sitting next to me — Queen Amina — doesn't do any actual governing either (her country is in Africa).

But still. A queen thinks I'm good at drawing!!!

We get an hour and a half for lunch at the RGA, and the food is very, very delicious. There are menus and waiters, and we can order whatever we want (within reason).

The only downside is that there is randomly assigned seating. That's so no 'friend groups' can be formed, because Madame Alain thinks royals should be 'friends with everyone'.

That's how today I got to sit next to Queen Amina.

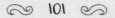 101

I knew it was rude to be drawing at the table while waiting for my food to be served (especially while sitting next to a queen), but I was doing it out of desperation because Luisa was telling a very long and boring story about what she was going to wear to my sister's wedding (after Luisa changes out of her bridesmaid gown, which Luisa says she's going to do as soon as our duties at the ceremony are over).

I've never heard of a bridesmaid changing out of her bridesmaid dress for the reception — even a junior bridesmaid. But Luisa says that it's quite normal in America.

I said, 'Well, I'm from America, and I've never heard of that.'

Luisa said, 'Kee-yow, Your Highness,' and started laughing.

So then I took out my notebook and said nothing. She is so annoying!

That's when Queen Amina leaned over to ask me, 'How long have you been drawing, Princess Olivia? You're quite good at it.'

I couldn't believe it! I was freaking out. Not only

is Queen Amina a queen, and very beautiful, but she's a high school boarding student, and very tall. She is about six foot two and on the RGA football team (which is co-ed). According to the rumours, she scored twenty-seven points against The Royal Academy in Switzerland (TRAIS), the RGA's fiercest rival.

'I've been drawing all my life,' I squeaked. 'Thank you so much, Your Royal Majesty!'

In the dining room we're supposed to address one another by proper title. But they're all so hard to remember:

- King or Queen — Your Majesty
- Prince or Princess — Your Highness
- Duke or Duchess — Your Grace
- Earl or Countess — Lord or Lady
- Baron or Baroness — also Lord or Lady
- Everyone else — Sir or Ma'am

'May I show your drawing to the rest of the table?' Queen Amina asked.

I nearly choked. 'Yes, Your Majesty, you may.'

I couldn't believe it! A queen liked my drawing enough to show it to other people!!!

'Cool drawing,' said several of them.

All except Luisa. She looked mad, probably because her boring story got cut off.

'Excuse me,' Luisa said. 'Did I happen to mention that the gown I'm changing into for the reception is by Claudio, the hottest designer in Rome, and that it has a long skirt that is detachable, so it turns into a minidress when the dancing starts?'

'Wow,' I said. I felt a little bad, because I only have one dress for the entire wedding, and I'm the sister of the bride. Plus, the skirt doesn't detach.

'I know,' Luisa said, and ate some of her lobster tail, since our food had finally been served. 'It truly is on the cutting edge.'

'Pardon me, but may I see that?' Prince Khalil asked. He wasn't even sitting at our table. He was sitting at the table *next* to our table. But he was looking at my notebook, which the queen was still holding up. 'Is that an *iguana*?'

'Uh,' I said, embarrassed for him that he couldn't

tell a kangaroo from an iguana. One is a mammal, and the other is a reptile. 'No. It's a kangaroo.'

'No, on the *other* side.'

Sure enough, it turned out there was a sketch of Carlos on the next page, the one turned towards him. I'd totally forgotten about it.

Then I felt embarrassed for *myself*.

'Oh,' I said, blushing. 'Yes, that's an iguana.'

'You like iguanas?'

I didn't want to say no, since he seemed so excited, so instead I said, 'Well . . . some of them.'

This wasn't a lie. I do like one iguana . . . Carlos. Sometimes I leave him strawberries I save from my breakfast plate, with the stems cut off.

'Did you know iguanas are amongst the most endangered species in the world?' Prince Khalil asked.

'No,' I said, surprised. 'I did not know that. We have a lot of them at the palace.'

'You do?' Prince Khalil looked amazed. 'They're not native to this area.'

'No,' I said. 'I know. My dad says someone probably

released a pair near the Royal Genovian Gardens, and now they, um . . .' I decided it was probably better not to go into detail about all the iguana babies.

But it turned out I didn't have to, since Prince Khalil already knew. He nodded excitedly. 'Iguanas make excellent pets, because they're very social, laid-back, and can live for up to twenty years.'

'Wow,' I said. 'That's a long time. We actually have so many that we'd like to get rid of them.'

'Well,' he said, still looking excited, 'I could probably—'

'Khalil, please!' Luisa cried. Her nostrils were getting very pinched. My pony Chrissy's nostrils flare when she's nervous or upset, but Luisa's nostrils get smaller when she feels this way. 'No one wants to hear facts about lizards while they're trying to eat their lunch!'

'Um,' I said. 'I don't mind, Luisa. It's kind of interesting — OW!'

The OW was because Luisa had kicked me under the table.

'No, it's *not* interesting, Princess Olivia,' she said.

'Oh,' I said. My ankle throbbed. Luisa wears very high-heeled shoes. 'I guess it's not interesting.'

'*I* find it interesting,' Queen Amina said.

Luisa looked like she'd bitten into a lemon or something all of a sudden. Her eyes got squinty and her mouth shrivelled up into the size of a grape.

'I'm so sorry, Your Majesty,' she said politely. 'Of course. Lizards are very interesting.'

Ha! HA HA HA HA HA!

But then one of the waiters arrived with the dessert cart . . . really, a trolley piled high with all different kinds of desserts, from which we get to pick whatever we want. There's pretty much every sort of dessert you can think of, from cream puffs to chocolate layer cake, plus delicious ripe fruit, too, if you want to be healthy.

So everyone forgot what we were talking about and concentrated on picking out what they wanted for dessert. I picked out the chocolate mousse because that's my favourite.

I guess the RGA isn't really that bad, except for the singing. And the dancing. And some of the people, particularly the Flexer, who is still flexing. I haven't thought of a way to make him stop. I'm starting to lose all feeling in my fingers.

This could become a problem for my future career as a wildlife illustrator. It's hard to draw when you have no feeling in your fingertips.

Tuesday 16 June
8.30 p.m.
Royal Genovian Bedroom

Nishi finally texted me back. But it wasn't a very nice text.

< NishiGirl

> My mom wants to know if she should bring her tennis racket or if you have extra ones at the palace that she can use. Write back soon, we're almost done packing.

> I hope you're not too princessy now to remember your old friends.

Why is she accusing me of being princessy? I'm the least princessy person I know! I'm way less princessy than the other girls at the Royal Genovian Academy (besides Komiko, who hardly ever talks, so it's nearly impossible to tell what she's like).

And why is being princessy even a bad thing? My sister is a princess, and she's great! She found housing for all the war refugees who've come here, and Genovia is the smallest country in Europe!

(And OK, the housing is on cruise ships. But that's only temporary. Who wouldn't want to live on a cruise ship? I would. Cruise ships have huge swimming pools with slides.)

Of course, we still don't have room for all the wedding guests who've said they're coming. At dinner tonight we got the latest count from Vivianne, the director of Palace Affairs, and she said that even though we only sent out 500 invitations, we've had over 550 replies saying yes!

That's more than the maximum number of people allowed in the ballroom! The fire marshal isn't going to be very happy.

'It's all the fault of that Bianca Ferrari,' Grandmère said. 'She must be making copies of the reception tickets, then handing them out to all her friends.'

'She can't,' Michael said. 'I made sure the tickets were printed with special holograms so they couldn't be reproduced . . . unless of course Bianca Ferrari has a 3-D holographic printer.'

'I wouldn't put anything past that woman!' Grandmère sniffed.

Mia's friend Lilly, who is also Michael's sister, said, 'Who cares? Just throw some extra tables and chairs in the garden. People can always grab a cocktail and a plate of appetizers and mingle around the pool.'

Grandmère looked horrified. 'Mingle? At a formal royal wedding reception banquet?'

'I think it will be *fine*,' said Mia's mom. 'At the weddings I go to in Brooklyn, the feeling is always the more the merrier.'

'This is Genovia, my dear,' Grandmère said, looking horrified. 'Not *Brooklyn*.'

'But have these extra people been vetted by the Royal Genovian Guard?' Mia's other friend Tina asked worriedly.

Dad looked up from his mobile. 'Good question. Have they?'

'Don't worry about it,' Mia's mom said, laying a hand on Dad's arm. 'It's going to be fine. Just fine.' The job of the mother of the bride is to tell everyone that everything is going to be just fine. Helen Thermopolis is very good at this.

'Of course, Your Highness,' Vivianne said. 'Security is our utmost concern. Everything will be taken care of.'

That's what she *said*.

But only because Mia was there, and you're not supposed to stress out a royal bride who has just taken over the throne and is pregnant with twins.

In reality, *nothing* is taken care of! And when my sister isn't around, *everyone* is FREAKING OUT.

○ The contractor who is installing the stage where Boris P, the internationally famous rock star, is supposed to play for the reception says there are not enough plugs for all the equipment Boris P and his band are bringing with them, and that the whole thing is so rickety, it's going to collapse as soon as Boris P steps on to it.

o Mia's friends Lilly and Lana say this is OK because Boris P used to go out with Tina, but he cheated on her with another girl. So now Lilly and Lana hate him and think it would be great if the stage collapsed while he was performing on it.

But Shameeka and Ling Su, Mia's other friends (and her other bridesmaids), say this *wouldn't* be great because Boris P (and others) could be seriously hurt, plus it would ruin the reception. And also there's reason to believe that Boris P *didn't* actually cheat. It could all simply be a misunderstanding.

So now the bridesmaids are arguing — only quietly, amongst themselves, since none of them want Mia to find out, because she's 'stressed' enough.

Except for Mia's friend Perin. She says she is staying out of it.

And Tina, of course, since she doesn't know about it.

- Chef Bernard says it's going to be humanly impossible to find enough European spiny lobsters for everyone at such short notice.
- The king of Lesotho wants to bring his new pet monkey with him, because it needs round-the-clock feeding, and the housekeeping staff is *not* too happy about that.
- There was a typo on the commemorative stamps, and instead of saying *HRH Prince Michael*, they say *HRH Prince Michele*, so now they all have to be destroyed and reprinted.

Grandmère's the only one not freaking out (except about the possibility of guests having to mingle outside). She showed me the new purple napkins that just arrived today, and they're *much* better than the boring cream-coloured ones my sister asked for. She's going to be so surprised.

'Nice job, Grandmère,' I said. We have to meet in secret in my bedroom so Mia won't overhear and have the surprise ruined. 'Also, just to let you know, I found out today that iguanas are endangered.'

'Not in my garden, they aren't!'

'I know. But you can't shoot at them, even to frighten them into moving to Bianca Ferrari's garden. You can't make your problem someone else's responsibility.'

She raised her eyebrows. 'Where did you hear *that*?'

'From *you*, Grandmère. You said that's what Dad is doing by making Mia take on the throne, when ruling is supposed to be his responsibility.'

Grandmère coughed. 'Oh. Well, perhaps you're right. But we're going to have to do *something* about those hideous creatures, Olivia. With all of those people coming, someone is bound to trip over one of them and end up in the pool.'

I thought about it. 'I know. But we still have a few days.'

'Four. *Four* days.'

'That's a long time,' I said. 'A lot can happen in four days. I started out an average girl one day, and I was a princess by the end of it.'

Grandmère looked at the ceiling. 'Very well. Goodnight, Olivia.'

'Goodnight, Grandmère.'

I just wrote Nishi back:

OlivGrace >

> We have lots of tennis rackets your mom can use, but since we're sending the private plane for you, I don't see why she can't bring hers. There's tons of room.

> And stop calling me princessy! I'm a princess, and proud to be one, but I'm not snobby. If princessy is supposed to be an insult, it isn't a very good one, because princesses are awesome. Can't wait to see you and show you around the palace. XOXOXOX

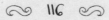

The majordomo is upset again. Today while I was at school, he caught Snowball on top of the gift table, eating a gingerbread castle given to Mia and Michael as a wedding present by some schoolchildren in Germany. Snowball had licked most of the gumdrop windows off.

She is out of control! I don't know what to do about it, other than locking her in my room all day.

But that seems cruel. She loves visiting with the staff and doing tricks for the tourists.

If only I could keep her away from the kitchen. And my sister's wedding gifts.

Here is my worst nightmare:

Wednesday 17 June
9.25 a.m.
Royal Genovian Academy
Madame Alain's Office

I just made a huge mistake.

No, not huge. HUMONGOUS.

But it's my own fault, I guess. I have no one to blame but myself.

It started when I walked into class this morning and saw that there was a folded-up note sitting on my desk. I knew it was for me because on the outside it said:

To HRH Olivia Grace

HRH means Her Royal Highness.

'Oooh, Olivia,' Marguerite teased. 'A love letter!'

Obviously she was joking. No one would leave a love letter on my desk (except maybe as a prank).

And it turns out I was right. When I opened up the note, I saw that inside was a drawing of a girl . . .

But not just any girl!

Me!

I could tell because she had glasses and big, curly hair pulled back by a headband. Only the headband had been made into a tiara (which I do not wear to school). Plus the girl in the drawing was wearing an RGA school uniform with shorts, just like mine.

But unlike me, the girl in the drawing had a really, really big butt.

That was my first clue that the 'artist' (I am using quotes around the word *artist* because I don't think the person who drew it is really an artist) was Prince Gunther, or at least someone *pretending* to be Prince Gunther, who is known for giving the people in his drawings, like Madame Alain, large butts.

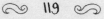

Except that coming out of the mouth of the girl in the drawing on my desk was a text bubble that said:

Hi, I'm the princess of Genovia, my sister is getting married and I think I'm so great, but I can't dance and I look stupid and I smell. Ha ha ha kee-yow LOL!

Only personally I didn't think there was anything to 'laugh out loud' about at all. In fact, when I saw the drawing, I got so mad, I could feel my face turning red, although I tried not to let how angry I was show in front of everyone else.

But it didn't work, since Marguerite asked, 'What's wrong? What does it say, Olivia?'

'Nothing,' I said, and quickly shoved the note in my backpack.

Only I wasn't quick enough, because Marguerite snatched the note out of my hand.

Then the next thing I knew, she was looking at it and saying, 'Oh, whoa! This is really rude. What does "kee-yow" mean?'

'Nothing!' I yelled. 'Never mind! Give it back!'

'Oh, I think it means *something*,' Luisa said with a laugh.

She would know.

I tried to snatch the note back, but of course Marguerite wouldn't give it up, because Victorine and the other girls were crying, 'Let *me* see! Let *me* see!'

And then the *worst thing ever happened*.

And that is that Prince Khalil came over and snatched the drawing out of Marguerite's hand and held it high over *all* our heads, which he could do easily because he's so tall.

'Noooo!' Luisa yelled. 'Don't look at it, Your Highness!'

Saying that had the opposite result Luisa was hoping for, though. Because once you tell someone *not* to do something, it automatically makes them want to do it more . . . like telling Rocky not to throw things down the stairs from the fourth floor. He simply can't help it. And neither could Prince Khalil.

As soon as his gaze fell on the page, he frowned.

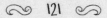

'"Kee-yow"?' he said. 'That's not a word.'

Then he turned the note around for *everyone* to see!

'Who drew this?' he asked. 'It isn't very nice. Gunther, this looks like one of your drawings. Did you do it?'

When everyone else saw it, they started to laugh . . . not in a mean way, exactly. I don't think they were laughing at *me*. They were laughing at the *drawing* and how dumb it was. I don't think anyone here really thinks I smell or have a humongous butt.

Except my cousin Luisa. Probably.

But I'm starting to think the same of her.

Gunther yelled, 'No! This I did not do! I draw much better than this!'

Which is actually a kind of funny thing to say, if you think about it.

'Oh, Gunther,' Luisa said, shaking her head. 'Obviously you did it. Look, it's your drawing style *exactly*. Why must you be so immature? And so hurtful to Olivia, Genovia's newest princess?'

I was so mad when she said this, I wanted to scream. It got even worse when Prince Khalil shook his head and said, 'Not cool, Gunther. Not cool.'

Gunther's eyes actually filled with tears. I didn't even know Gunther *had* feelings, I'd been so busy being grossed out by him.

But I guess it would hurt my feelings, too, if the tallest, cutest boy in the sixth grade told me I wasn't cool.

'No!' Gunther wailed. 'This I did not do! I know I draw Madame Alain with the big butt. But not this! This I did not draw!'

'You did it, Gunther,' Luisa said. 'And we all know it. So you might as well admit it.'

But I knew Gunther *didn't* do it, because *Luisa's* the only one who ever says 'kee-yow' (except for me, but I only did it once, by mistake).

I don't know why she'd do something so mean. Maybe because Queen Amina said she liked my drawings and didn't pay enough attention to her boring story about her reception gown with the detachable skirt?

Or maybe because her *pretend* boyfriend doesn't really like her?

Oh yes, I said it! I said Khalil is Luisa's pretend boyfriend, because I haven't seen any proof yet that Prince Khalil even likes her!

But whatever. I know Luisa did it! And what Luisa was doing — accusing Gunther of drawing that picture, when I knew he didn't — wasn't fair!

'Luisa,' I started to say. 'Why don't you just—'

But right then Monsieur Montclair came into the classroom, a mug of steaming coffee in his hands. 'Ladies and gentlemen, what is all this shouting? I could hear you down the hallway. You are hardly deporting yourself like young royals.'

'Look what Prince Gunther did, Monsieur!' Luisa cried, showing him the drawing.

'No,' Gunther said desperately. 'I did not do it!'

Monsieur Montclair took one look at the picture and said with a tired sigh, 'Prince Gunther, please go and pay a visit to Madame Alain in her office. The rest of you, get in your dance positions. Mademoiselle Justine is on her way.'

I saw Prince Gunther's face crumple.

'No!' he said. 'This is third strike for me! Madame Alain said if I get one more strike, I have to go back to Stockerdörfl. Then my parents will put me in The Royal Academy in Switzerland.'

Everyone gasped in horror at the idea of an RGA student having to attend horrible TRAIS. Meanwhile, Gunther picked up his backpack and walked glumly towards the door, his head hanging.

'Well, auf Wiedersehen, everyone,' he said.

I felt so bad for him! He isn't my favourite person or anything. He isn't even in my top fifty favourite people.

But I don't hate him or think it's fair for him to get in trouble for something he didn't do.

'Luisa,' I whispered, poking her, 'I know it was you who made that drawing! Why would you do that?'

'To help you, of course,' she said, looking wide-eyed with innocence. 'Now you don't have to worry about the Flexer. You don't even have to learn the steps to the dance, because you don't have to be in it,

since you don't have a partner any more. See?' She smiled. 'I'm a true royal, just like your sister, who everyone says is going to save Genovia from economic ruin. *Prego*, Olivia.'

Prego means *You're welcome* in Italian. Uggggh!

'Luisa, when I need your help, I'll ask for it, OK?' I raised my hand. 'Uh, Monsieur Montclair, may I be excused?'

He sipped his coffee, looking very bored. 'Yes, Princess Olivia, you may be excused, but next time remember to use the bathroom before class begins, OK?'

More ugghhh! Why did he have to bring up the bathroom in front of everyone? Like Prince Khalil? Hadn't I been humiliated enough in one morning?

Anyway, I'm in Madame Alain's office now . . . or really, the waiting room to her office, where her assistant is playing a video game on his computer but pretending like he's working.

Prince Gunther was totally surprised to see me, which I can understand, seeing as how everyone else thinks he drew a mean picture of me.

'Princess Olivia,' he said. 'What are you doing here?'

'I know it wasn't you who drew that picture, Gunther,' I said.

'But . . . but . . . how?' he asked.

I didn't want to say *Because only my cousin Luisa says kee-yow*, because that would be tattling on Luisa.

Instead I said, 'I just do. When Madame Alain gets here, I'll tell her so.'

Prince Gunther looked even more surprised. 'You . . . you *will*? Why would you do this for me?'

I couldn't believe he didn't know. 'Because, Gunther. This is royalty school. We're supposed to do the right thing. I mean, even if we weren't royal, we're still supposed to tell the truth. And the truth is, you didn't do it.'

Gunther looked down at his lap. I thought I saw disappointment on his face. 'Oh,' he said. 'I thought . . . I thought maybe you liked me or something.'

EWWWWWWWWWW!!!! The Flexer thinks I like him!!!!!!!!!!!!!!

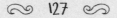

This is the reward you get for trying to be nice: A green-haired, bogey-flinging prince will think that you like him.

Then it got even worse. Because after I got over trying not to die, I said, 'Uh, well, it's not that, exactly, Gunther. It's just that . . .'

'Because,' Prince Gunther looked up to say, 'I *really* like you. You're not like the other girls in this school.'

I did not like the way this conversation was going. 'Well, Gunther, that's very nice, but—'

'Yes. You're like me.' He showed me his shower sandals and kneesocks. 'You aren't afraid to be different. You wear shorts. And glasses. You don't care what people say. I think that's cool.'

UGGHHH! The Flexer thinks I like him, and even worse, the Flexer likes me back because he thinks I like to take fashion risks (which I do, but mostly because I like to dress for comfort, unless I'm attending an important state function)!

No! No, no, no!

I'm trying to remember what Grandmère and my

sister told me to say in these kinds of situations. Surely there has to be some sort of rule that royals follow when someone says they like them but they don't like that person back. What's the right thing to say in return?

Thanks, but no thanks? That seems rude.

Thanks, but I just want to be friends? That seems better.

The sad part is, Grandmère and I have never talked about what I should say if a green-haired, bogey-flinging prince tells me that he likes me — and thinks I like him back!

Because this is not a situation I ever imagined would happen!

AHHHHHHHHH!!!!!

Wednesday 17 June
11.25 a.m.
Royal Genovian Academy

Phew! Thank goodness *that's* over.

Though now I'm actually worse off than before, really. Grandmère says when you're in a bad situation and you make a poor decision that only puts you in a worse situation, it's called 'jumping from the frying pan into the fire'.

(Though whenever she says this, Dad always laughs and says, 'Mother, when have *you* ever cooked?')

Still, that's what I've just done with Prince

Gunther . . . jumped from the frying pan into the fire.

I was getting all ready to say the politest thing I could think of — which was:

'Well, Gunther, I do like you — as a FRIEND' — when the door to Madame Alain's office opened and she finally came in from her meeting (except that I noticed she had a lot of shopping bags. Genovia is known for its fine shopping, so I can understand, but I'm not sure it's right for the head of a school — even a school for modern young royals — to go shopping during school hours).

So then I couldn't give my speech to Gunther because instead I had to tell Madame Alain that there'd been a terrible mistake and that Prince Gunther was innocent.

'I don't know,' Madame Alain said, looking down at the drawing, which Monsieur Montclair had given to the administrative assistant to give to her as evidence of Gunther's crime. 'It certainly LOOKS like Prince Gunther's work.'

'Well, it's not,' I said, horribly aware the whole

time that Prince Gunther was staring at me with big lovey-dovey hearts in his eyes, probably planning OUR royal wedding.

'Princess Olivia,' Madame Alain said, 'I know you're only trying to protect your new classmate because you want to fit in and don't care to make waves your first week. But I can assure you that this isn't the first time Prince Gunther has done something like this. He's been warned that if he did it again, he'd be expelled.'

'But I didn't do it!' Gunther cried, turning his big moon eyes on Madame Alain.

'Prince Gunther,' Madame Alain said, holding his drawing towards him. 'Please don't lie. It isn't becoming of your royal status. Your father would be very disappointed in you. Now, this is obviously your work.'

'It isn't his work, Madame Alain,' I said. I'm afraid I had to do something very unroyal. I took a deep breath and lied: 'It's mine.'

Madame Alain stared at me in shock. '*Yours*? Are

you saying you drew this of *yourself*, Princess Olivia?'

'Yes.' I opened this journal and showed her some of my sketches. 'You see? I love to draw. I drew that picture of myself, Madame Alain, for exactly the reason you said . . . to make the other girls in my class laugh, since I want to fit in. You know I haven't been a royal for as long as some of the other students, and I only wanted to make them like me.'

'*I* like you,' Prince Gunther said.

Ugh!!!! Thanks for *not* helping, Gunther. I ignored him.

'Please, please don't tell my father, Madame Alain,' I said. 'Or my sister. You can tell my grandmother, though. She won't mind.'

'Oh, Your Highness!' Madame Alain looked even more shocked. 'This is . . . well, this is terrible. If you didn't feel that you were fitting in, you should have come to me! You know that I'm available to talk at any time, don't you?'

Um, except when she's busy shopping.

'Thank you, Madame Alain,' I said. 'That's good to know. Can we go back to class now, please? We need to rehearse. I want to make sure that our wedding surprise for my sister and Prince Michael is perfect.'

'Of course!' Madame Alain stood up and shook my hand. 'And please, if there's anything else I can do to make your time at the Royal Genovian Academy more pleasant, do not hesitate to let me know.'

'Uh,' I said. 'OK, Madame Alain. I will.'

Phew! Boy, was I glad when we got out of there.

But then I had to deal with Prince Gunther, who was looking at me like I was the dessert trolley they wheel around at lunch. This was not a very comfortable feeling.

'Princess, I can't believe you did that for me,' he said as we walked back to class. 'No one has *ever* done something so nice for me! People in this school . . . well, they don't seem to like me so much. I think they are jealous because of my guns. See?'

He pushed up the short sleeve of his uniform shirt to show me his muscle. AGAIN.

This time, however, I put a hand out to stop him.

'Yeah, OK, Gunther, look, I've seen your guns before. You show them to me all the time.'

He looked a little disappointed by my response, but he pushed his sleeve back down.

'I'm going to the Olympics,' he said. 'Because I'm such a good swimmer.'

'I know,' I said. 'You've said that, too. Gunther, you have to stop telling people that. It sounds really braggy.'

He froze in the middle of the corridor, which is open-air and filled with flower-covered vines and little tweeting birds.

'But it's the truth!' he cried. 'I *am* going to the Olympics!'

'Even if it's the truth,' I said, 'it's better to let people find out about your talents on their own than for you to go around bragging about them. And another thing: When you flex your arm when we're promenading, you cut off the blood supply to my fingertips.'

He looked confused. 'But girls like big muscles. I

train every day with the toughest coach in Genovia. He's from the Ukraine. He makes me lift twice my body weight.'

'That's great. But maybe save the flexing for the gym with your coach,' I said. 'Because if I show up at my sister's wedding with my hand in a cast, no one's going to be happy about it. And then when I tell them it was because of you, the Olympic Committee will find out about it, and you'll get in trouble.'

I had no idea if this was true, but it worked, since he said, looking a little shocked, 'I'm sorry. I guess I don't know my own strength.'

'I guess not. I probably should have told you earlier.'

'Yes,' he said. 'You must tell me right away if I do anything that is wrong, now that you are my girlfriend.'

WHAT????

'Gunther,' I said, 'I'm not your girlfriend. I'm just your friend, who is a girl.'

'No,' he said, reaching for my hand as we walked down the corridor towards the sixth-grade classroom. 'You rescued me from being expelled. You like me. I know you do! So now we are more than friends.'

'No,' I said, pulling my hand away. 'No, we are not. Just friends, Gunther. Just friends!'

He laughed like he thought I was making it up, or teasing him, or flirting, or something, which I was NOT!

UGGGHHHH!!!

Goodbye, frying pan. Hello, fire.

Wednesday 17 June
3.35 p.m.
Royal Genovian Stables

I'm hiding in the stables right now with Chrissy and Snowball because this is the only place people aren't rushing around setting up things or cleaning for the wedding, and I need to think. I have to get this all down or I'm going to go crazy. I can't believe this. My life is a nightmare!

And Nishi is coming TOMORROW, expecting me to be living some kind of fairy-tale princess life, and I'm so NOT!

Well, I mean, I kind of am, compared to most

people. My life is basically much, much better than it was. I don't want to seem ungrateful.

But this princess thing is *not* as easy as I thought it was going to be!

(Although I have to admit, the food really makes up for a lot of it. Oh, and the clothes. And having wonderful pets and living with people who actually care about me.)

But some of them care *too much*! Prince Gunther, for instance, who has now stopped flinging bogeys and making fart noises with his mouth, because he thinks if he acts more 'princely', I'll be his girlfriend.

Even though I have assured him (in the nicest way possible) that this is most definitely NOT TRUE! There is nothing he can do to make me want

him as a boyfriend. NOTHING. I only want to be friends.

I think tomorrow if he's still acting so lovey-dovey, I might have to ask my dad if I can be homeschooled . . . or transferred to The Royal School in Switzerland. I don't want to hurt Gunther's feelings or anything (I already had to watch him cry once today).

But I do NOT want Prince Gunther as a boyfriend. Not because of his socks and shower sandals or green hair or anything like that. I just do NOT like him in that way.

But of course as soon as we got back to class and started dancing again, Luisa noticed how he was treating me (seriously, no one could miss it: He now handles me as if I were a dainty leaf that he might crush with the slightest touch) and leaned over to whisper, while we were promenading, 'Kee-yow, Olivia! I think *someone* has a crush!'

Since this whole thing was Luisa's fault anyway, I gave her a dirty look and whispered back, 'Not helping, Luisa.'

'Why?' She pretended I'd hurt her feelings, which I know I hadn't, because Lady Luisa has no feelings. 'Now you can invite him to your sister's wedding reception. You want to have someone to dance with there, too, don't you?'

ACK!

'Still not helping, Luisa!' I said when I passed her again on the next promenade.

She only laughed and flounced away.

At least I'm not the only one who notices. Luisa is so mean that even Princess Komiko, who hardly ever says anything, whispered to me at lunch today, 'Don't let Lady Luisa get you down, Princess. She's rude to everyone.'

'But why?' I asked as we practised using our fish forks. 'She's so pretty. Why does she have to be so mean?'

'She didn't used to be,' Princess Komiko said. 'But then her parents got divorced.'

I almost choked on my endive salad. 'Her parents got divorced?'

'Yes,' Princess Komiko said. 'In the second grade.

After that, she became very rude. Of course, my parents got divorced, too, but I did not become rude to everyone. I guess it can affect different people in different ways. Would you please pass the salt?'

I passed Princess Komiko the salt, thinking about what she'd said. Luisa's parents were divorced? That was terrible! I've never had divorced parents, so I don't know what it feels like. I have a dead mother, but she died when I was a baby and I'd never got a chance to know her. It's certainly true that things affect different people in different ways.

But no one should take their problems out on other people.

See, this is why I'd never been as big a fan of fairy tales as Nishi — especially ones with princesses in them. She completely believes that when it says 'And they lived happily ever after' at the end, that's it, that's the end, and everyone really does live happily ever after.

But that's not true. Life keeps on happening after the end. Good stuff *and* bad stuff. You could be a princess like Komiko and have your parents get divorced. Or you could be a princess like me and escape one mean girl (like Annabelle, at my old school) only to find another one (my cousin Luisa) at your new school.

Who (besides Nishi) even believes in fairy tales, anyway? Some of those stories are all right, I guess, like 'Little Red Riding Hood'. It's never a good idea to talk to strangers, especially wolves.

But some of those other stories don't even make any sense. It's not physically possible to sleep for a hundred years! You would die of starvation.

And princes can't really kiss anyone awake (unless what they're really doing is performing CPR).

Whenever I bring this up, though, Nishi says I'm missing the point, and that all of these things are happening due to magic, and that I'm just not ready yet to see the magic in real life.

But I *have* seen magic in real life! I went from living in the suburbs of New Jersey to a castle in Genovia, didn't I?

So what's Nishi going to say when she gets here and she finds out I'm messing everything up, and maybe — possibly — ruining everyone's happily ever after?

And OK, maybe that's a little bit of an exaggeration — nobody has bitten any poisoned apples and died or anything.

But I don't feel as if my plan of helping Mia with her problems as a wedding gift is really working out, in part due to my cousin Luisa, who has problems of her own.

Instead I'm only creating *more* problems . . . especially since this afternoon when I got home from school, the majordomo told me that Snowball had stolen two sausages and wheel of Brie from the kitchen today!

A group of tourists found part of the Brie later in the Hall of Portraits. It was behind the bust of my great-great-grandfather. The tourists took photos of it and now 'Dog Cheese' is one of the top trending topics online.

I wish I could just live here in the stables with Chrissy and Snowball. Everything is so calm and nice and smells like hay.

Which is quite a good smell, when you get used to it.

But as I explained to Rocky when he wanted to fly to the moon, you can't run away from your problems . . . You have to face them, or they'll never get solved.

So I have to go back to school tomorrow and face everyone — including Luisa.

And Prince Gunther.

Oh, there's Grandmère out there with the electricians, telling them where to string the party lights for the reception. I guess I should go and help.

Wednesday 17 June
7.35 p.m.
Royal Genovian Bedroom

!!!!!

WOW.

☺☺☺☺☺☺☺☺☺☺☺

OK, maybe things are looking up. Just a little.

I was outside helping the electricians swap out the white party globes for purple ones (which has to be done in secret. Grandmère says it will be a great surprise for Mia to see everyone and everything bathed in soft purple light) when I was the one who got a surprise.

Prince Khalil showed up in the Royal Genovian Gardens!

'What are *you* doing here?' I asked from on top of my ladder.

'What are *you* doing here?' he asked from below it.

'I live here,' I said.

'Right,' he said with a laugh. 'Sorry, I knew that. What I meant was . . . what are you doing way up there?'

'Oh,' I said. 'Helping to hang party lights for my sister's wedding reception. It's in two days and basically nothing is ready, so I'm pitching in to help.'

I could have given him a longer explanation — like how earlier Grandmère had told me another rule for royals: 'Better to do it yourself than trust other people to do it, so you know it's done right' — but I suddenly remembered that I was wearing my uniform shorts, and I wasn't sure whether or not he could see up them, so I started climbing down.

I was surprised when he reached over to hold the bottom rungs of the ladder to steady it, but I shouldn't

have been. This kind of courteousness is why Luisa has such a crush on him.

'Thanks,' I said as I jumped the last few feet to the garden path. My pink high-tops made a satisfying crunching sound on the gravel.

'No problem,' he said. 'Hey, I'm glad we ran into each other. About what happened in school today—'

Oh, no! This was the *last* thing I wanted to talk about! Especially with him.

'Uh-oh,' I said. 'Did you hear that? I think my grandmother is calling me. It's probably time for high tea. Sorry, I have to go.'

'Wait.' Prince Khalil reached out to grab my arm. 'I just wanted to say that I think it was cool how you said you drew that picture so that Prince Gunther wouldn't get kicked out of school.'

I froze. 'You did? I mean, you do?'

'Yeah.' He let go of my arm. 'Not many girls would have done that.'

I was shocked, and not only because Prince Khalil had just grabbed my arm and said I was cool, but because he'd ACTUALLY NOTICED SOMETHING I'D DONE.

Not that I cared.

'Uh,' I said. Suddenly it seemed like all the birds

in the garden were tweeting more loudly than usual, and the sun was shining a little more brightly, which makes no sense because I do not even like Prince Khalil. 'Well, Prince Gunther didn't draw that picture. So I was only doing the right thing.'

'Yeah,' Prince Khalil said. 'But *you* didn't draw it.'

This conversation was making me very uncomfortable, because the last thing I wanted to be discussing with Prince Khalil was who really drew the picture, which of course was Luisa Ferrari, who secretly wanted to be his girlfriend.

'Well,' I said. 'Maybe not. But it still wouldn't have been fair if Prince Gunther got kicked out of school for something he didn't do.'

'No,' Prince Khalil said. 'But if *he* didn't draw it, and *you* didn't draw it, who did?'

'Uh.' I thought it better to distract him. 'What's *that*?' I pointed at the wire cage Prince Khalil had put down while holding the ladder for me, then lifted again.

'Oh, this?' It worked! My trick worked! He held

up the cage so I could take a better look at it. 'It's a live trap. I'm a volunteer with the Genovian Herpetology Rescue Society. We're here today to trap and relocate your iguanas.'

It was a good thing I'd climbed down from the ladder, or I would have fallen off it. 'You *are*?'

'Yeah,' Khalil said, his dark eyes lighting up the way they had in the school dining room. 'I told my friends at the society what you said about all the problems you were having here at the palace with iguana overcrowding, and they got in touch with the gardening and security staff, and they said we could come in and set up these traps. We're going to relocate as many of your iguanas as we can to the Genovian golf course. They'll be much happier there and won't bother anyone.'

'Wow,' I said. 'That's, uh, really nice of you.'

'Oh, it's nothing.' He shrugged modestly. 'The society is happy to help. Conserving reptiles and amphibians and educating the public about how critical they are to the environment is what we do.

Did you know that without many species of reptiles, some plants wouldn't get pollinated, and certain pests would overrun the ecosystem?'

'Uh,' I said. 'No, I didn't.'

'Well, it's true. Where can I put this?' He held out the wire cage.

'Over here,' I said, and led him to the orange tree beneath my bedroom window. I couldn't see Carlos anywhere, but I knew he was around. Sometimes he hides. 'You're going to need a lot of those, though.'

'I know,' he said. 'That's why we came today. We'll set as many traps as we can now, and then keep coming back. By the wedding we should have got most of them.'

The birds in the trees seemed to tweet even more loudly. 'This is going to be the best wedding present for my sister,' I said. 'I've been wondering what I was going to get her, since I don't have any money.'

He smiled. 'I never heard of anyone giving someone iguana removal for their wedding before, but I guess it would make a pretty good gift, and not just because it's free. I'd love to be an iguana removal specialist when I grow up, because it makes people so happy, and it's great for the iguanas.' Then the grin turned into a frown. 'Only I can't, of course.'

I felt a pang for him, since he looked so sad. 'Why not? Don't they have iguanas in your native land?'

He looked at me like I was crazy. 'No, because I have to be a prince.'

'Oh, right,' I said, embarrassed. 'Of course! I can't believe I forgot.' I'd also forgotten that his native land was in the middle of a war, and this was why he was a boarding student at the RGA and his parents lived in France. Probably it had been insensitive of me to have brought it up. I decided to change the subject. 'You know, I want to be a wildlife illustrator. I think it's possible to be both . . . royal and something else. Most people do more than one thing.'

'You know what,' he said, after crawling from the live trap, which he'd finished setting up. 'I never thought about it before, but you're right. Like Prince Gunther. He's royal, but he's also a swimmer.'

 153

I didn't like how our conversations always seemed to go back to Prince Gunther, especially since I don't even like Prince Gunther . . . at least, not the way Prince Gunther likes me.

But since making a big deal about it would only make it seem like I do, I said, 'Yes, just like Prince Gunther.'

'Well,' Prince Khalil said, looking at the trap. 'That's something to think about. Anyway, one down. About a hundred more to go.'

I felt so grateful and happy that he'd come along out of nowhere and been so nice, I wanted to do something nice for him . . . only I couldn't think what. Warning him about Luisa's plan to make him her boyfriend at the wedding reception ball and dance with him in the moonlight and force him to give up his love of herpetology didn't seem appropriate.

Maybe he *wants* to be Luisa's boyfriend. I don't know.

So instead I just said, 'Well, I'll let you get to work, then. Thanks a lot. If you or any of your friends from the herpetology society want to come inside for an orange juice or something, find me and let me know!'

'OK.' He smiled. How come I never noticed before what a nice smile he has? 'Thanks. See you later.'

'See you later.'

Somehow as I was backing away from the orange tree I managed not to trip over any roots or anything. I don't know how.

Reading this over, I know it seems as if I like Prince Khalil, but I swear I don't! He's very nice and everything, but I have enough problems without crushing on a prince, especially a prince who happens to be my cousin Luisa's crush.

But let's just say if I *were* going to have a crush on a prince, it would probably be on Prince Khalil. He has very good manners and nice eyes and he's kind to iguanas.

But I don't. At *all*.

Thursday 18 June
8.30 a.m.
Royal Genovian Bedroom

When I woke up this morning, I looked out into the garden and every cage had an iguana inside! Well, almost every one. It looks like Carlos has 'evaded capture' (as Rocky likes to say, when he forces me to play Astronaut Versus the Velociraptor with him).

I can't wait to tell Prince Khalil!!!!!

Not about Carlos. About the other iguanas.

Of course, Prince Khalil didn't give me his mobile number, so I have to wait until I get to school.

But this is very exciting!

Although I can't say that I ever expected I'd be excited to tell a boy — much less a prince — about a bunch of captured lizards in my yard.

No one else has noticed the cages except Rocky and Grandmère, because everyone else in my family is still asleep. Even more of Mia's friends (and Michael's entire family) arrived yesterday. I could hear them laughing and singing *all night* long, practically, after I went to bed. When I peeked out of my window, I saw my sister and Michael doing this:

Weddings sure do make people happy, considering all the trouble everyone has to go to in order to have one.

Only Grandmère and Rocky were sitting at the breakfast table when I came down. She lowered her newspaper and asked, 'What in heaven's name is going on out there in the garden, Olivia? It looks like something out of a science-fiction movie, and not one I'd care to see.'

'*I'd* care to see it,' Rocky said.

'Those are live traps for the iguanas, Grandmère,' I said. 'Prince Khalil is a member of the Genovian Herpetology Rescue Society.'

I explained how Prince Khalil and his friends had set up the traps and planned to move the iguanas to the Genovian golf course.

'Pfuit,' she said. 'That should certainly be a surprise to the golfers. Well, be sure to thank Prince Khalil for me. Or perhaps when I see him, I'll give him a nice tip. Do you think ten euros would be enough? I suppose I should make it twenty. Or should I tip a euro per cage?'

'Oh no, Grandmère,' I said. 'The service is free. Conserving reptiles and amphibians and educating the public about them is all the thanks the society needs.'

Grandmère raised her eyebrows. But since they weren't painted on yet, you could barely tell.

'Not very enterprising of them . . . but then, I suppose the prince takes after his grandfather. Extremely intellectual, but terrible with money. That's how they failed to hang on to their fortune, you know.'

'I think Prince Khalil sounds cool,' Rocky said. '*I* want to join the Genovian Herpetology Rescue Society.'

Grandmère turned back to her newspaper. 'Why am I not surprised?'

Thursday 18 June
9.30 a.m.
Royal Limousine

Got the biggest jolt when I walked into class today:

Prince Gunther wasn't wearing kneesocks *or* shower shoes!!!

He was wearing long trousers, proper shoes, and his uniform tie, and his shirt was nicely ironed and tucked in, the sleeves rolled down so he wasn't showing off his 'guns'.

He actually looked . . . well, less horrible.

All the girls were buzzing about his transformation, even my cousin Luisa.

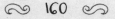

'This is because of you!' she ran over to whisper to me. For once, she didn't look angry. She looked excited. 'Gunther gave himself a makeover because *you* told him to!'

'Me?' I was confused. 'I never told him to—'

Then I remembered guiltily that I had. Sort of.

'Wait,' I said. 'I never told him to get a makeover. All I told him to do was to stop flinging bogeys and making fart noises. And flexing.'

'See!' Luisa looked triumphant. 'It *is* because of you!' She turned to Victorine and Marguerite. 'I told you. A man will do anything for the woman he loves!'

I felt a little sick. I hadn't meant for Gunther to stop wearing his shower shoes. Although I had to admit he looked — and smelt — a lot better. Those shower shoes were pretty old.

'I wish a boy would do something like that for me,' Victorine said with a sigh.

Marguerite agreed. 'I know, right? He's almost as cute as Prince Khalil!'

I expected Luisa to say something like 'How

dare you!' or 'No one could be as cute as my darling Khalil!'

But she didn't. She was staring at Prince Gunther and his makeover as moony-eyed as all the other girls!

I couldn't believe it.

Not that Prince Khalil even noticed, because he was busy reading yet another book about reptiles and amphibians. He barely looked up when I crept away from the other girls to tell him that the cages he and his friends had left were full this morning.

'Oh, cool,' he said. 'Some of the society members will be over to transport the iguanas to the golf course. Then they'll set the cages back up and see how many more we can catch.'

'Great!' I said. 'Thanks again for doing that.'

'I'm glad I could help.' He smiled, and even though I don't like him as anything but a friend, I have to admit I can see why Luisa likes him so much.

I was turning around to go back to my desk when *the worst thing happened.*

Prince Gunther came leaping forward, bowed, and held my chair out for me (the way gentlemen sometimes do for ladies, except NOT IN CLASS IN FRONT OF EVERYONE).

Then he said, 'Good morning, Your Royal Highness.'

AGGGHHHH.

But all the girls in class *loved* it. They giggled and clapped, even Princess Komiko. Even Luisa.

'Uh,' I said. 'Good morning, Prince Gunther.'

I pretty much wanted to die on the spot. Although Grandmère told me it is humanly impossible to die of embarrassment. Unfortunately.

'I hope you are having a lovely day,' Gunther said.

'I am,' I said. 'I hope you are, too.'

'I *am*,' he said.

'Great,' I said. He was leaning right over me! He wouldn't leave!

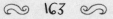

'Great,' he said. 'Do you notice anything different about me?'

'Yes,' I said. 'You aren't wearing shower shoes.'

'Yes,' he said. 'I did it for you.'

'Wow,' I said. 'That's nice. I think you should go sit down now. Monsieur Montclair is going to be here in a minute.'

'All right,' Prince Gunther said, and smiled really big. 'I'm very happy to see you this morning.'

'Great,' I said. 'But we're still just friends, remember?'

'Yes,' he said, still smiling. 'That's what you told me yesterday. I haven't forgotten. But you're my *first* friend at this school! No one else has ever been so nice to me. Last night on the telephone I told my parents about you, and they want to invite you to come to Stockerdörfl to visit us this summer.'

'Wow,' I said. 'That's great. We'll see.'

Grandmère says when you don't want to do something, just say, *Great. We'll see!* because that way you're not really saying yes or no. You're saying, *Actually, my schedule is quite busy and I*

have to check with my royal secretary. But I'll get
back to you quite soon.

'You will really enjoy Stockerdörfl,' Gunther
went on. 'We are known for our excellent skiing.'

Luisa overheard all this and started to laugh. 'I
bet Olivia's been skiing lots of times.'

She is such a pill.

'I haven't, actually,' I said. 'But I would love to
learn.'

No. Not really. I only have time for one hobby,
and that's drawing. I just said that because Luisa
was being so annoying.

But it was the wrong thing to say, because it made
Prince Gunther look excited.

'Really?' he asked. 'I could teach you to ski! I am
as good at skiing as I am at swimming!'

Oh no.

Then, thank GOODNESS, the door to the
classroom opened.

But instead of Monsieur Montclair walking in, it
was my bodyguard, Serena.

At first I thought she was there to tell Prince

Gunther to please back away slowly from me, because that's what bodyguards are trained to do.

But instead, she held out my mobile. We aren't allowed to carry our mobiles in school — unless we sneak them, like Luisa — and are instead supposed to leave them with our bodyguards, who are to contact us about calls if there is an emergency.

Which is what I thought there was when I saw Serena holding my mobile towards me. My heart gave a double flip, and I stood up.

'Oh no,' I said. 'Is there something wrong?'

Was it Dad? Had he had a heart attack from all the stress of the rising wedding costs and sinking foundation? Was it Grandmère? Had something gone wrong with the purple dye? Or was it something even worse . . . my sister, and the babies?

'No, no,' Serena said. 'It's your friend Nishi. Did you forget she's arriving today? She and her family just landed at the Genovian airport.'

Thursday 18 June
3.30 p.m.
Royal Pool

Nishi is here!!!!!

I can hardly believe it, but it's true, because she's sitting right next to me on a blue-and-white-striped sun lounger, in one of her five bathing suits, soaking up the Genovian sun (while wearing SPF 50 and a big sun hat and enormous sunglasses, sipping Genovian orange juice and petting Snowball).

We aren't fighting any more. I forgot what we were even fighting about.

When I saw her coming down the steps from the

plane, I ran across the airport tarmac and gave her the biggest hug, and she hugged me back. I don't think I've ever been so glad to see anyone in my entire life (except when I met my dad for the first time).

I'm the worst person. I can't believe I forgot Nishi and her family were coming today! Although I *have* had a few things on my mind.

Thank goodness Mia not only remembered but sent Serena to get me out of class.

I texted Mia from the limo on the way from the airport:

< HRH Princess Mia Thermopolis 'FtLouie'   OlivGrace >

> Can I really have the day off from school to hang out with Nishi???

Of course. It's what a gracious hostess should do! Although for some reason Madame Alain is insisting that you be in school tomorrow, which is definitely not going to work with our schedule.

Oops.

> Well, I sort of have to be in school from 11 a.m.–12 p.m. tomorrow. And you and Michael have to be there, too.

What? Why?

I can't tell you. It's a surprise.

But isn't it listed on your schedule?

My sister (and probably all people with jobs, not just princesses) gets a printed schedule at the beginning of the week, telling her exactly where she's supposed to be and what she's supposed to be doing almost every hour of every day, Monday to Sunday.

But like I've said, getting a party organized for 500 people — now 550 — is very difficult, although things are starting to come together! I noticed the under-butlers laying out all the silver this morning, and the contractors have finally finished building the stage for Boris P to perform on. It's definitely not going to collapse beneath him. All the bridesmaids — minus Tina — stood on it together and jumped on it up and down to make sure. Only Michael's sister Lilly looked disappointed when it didn't come crashing apart.

All I have on my schedule for 11 a.m. tomorrow is an appointment at the salon with Paolo. That's when all of us — you and Nishi, and Luisa, too! — are getting our manicures and pedicures before our final dress fittings, and then rehearsal.

Ouch! I should have known Dad had been so distracted with everything going on, he hadn't passed the message about our special performance from Madame Alain to Mia's office.

Mani-pedis! That would be great!

Not really. Not the part about Luisa being there. But I know I have to act like I like her, because she's my cousin and a fellow junior bridesmaid, and junior bridesmaids aren't supposed to fight. It's not about them and their personal feelings. It's about the bride!

But can we do the mani-pedis at a different time?

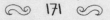

> Because there's something VERY SPECIAL going on at the RGA at that exact time. Dad said he put it on your calendar and that you knew about it.

> Something very special going on at the RGA? I'm curious! In that case, I suppose we can squeeze it in. Have fun with your friend!

> I will!

So now Nishi and I ARE having fun! The most fun I've had in a while.

It's so strange to see her here at the palace, sitting on the throne (the first thing she wanted to do), checking out the wedding gifts (they're being stacked up higher and higher), and spying on the tourists (we joined one of the tours and they didn't even realize who we were. Although it's true we were wearing *Visit Genovia!* baseball hats). She's posted a bunch of selfies of us online for the girls back home to see.

'They're going to be so jealous!' she keeps saying.

So I guess I was worried about her thinking I'm not living a fairy-tale life for nothing. She thinks everything is amazing. She loves Chrissy, my bedroom, and even my *closet*.

'Your closet is bigger than my whole bedroom,' she said. Which is true.

She's even more excited about the fact that while we were eating lunch, the housekeeping staff went into her room and unpacked her bags, ironed all her clothes, and hung everything up.

'Of course,' I said. 'They do that for everyone. Unless you bring a monkey.'

Nishi thinks I'm leading the most glamorous, amazing life in the whole world.

And I guess I can see why to her it would look like I am. She doesn't know about Prince Gunther wanting to be my boyfriend (not a good thing) or Luisa being so mean.

I could tell her, but why? After tomorrow, none

of it is going to matter any more, because school will be over for the summer. And I won't have to see any of those people again until the autumn (well, except for Prince Khalil and Luisa, Marguerite, and Victorine at the wedding).

But Luisa won't be able to be mean to me in front of Grandmère. And I sort of don't mind the idea of seeing Prince Khalil again.

If I can just get through the performance tomorrow, everything will be fine!

So I'm going to pretend like none of that is happening and be on holiday, like Nishi is, for the rest of the day.

Friday 19 June
11.00 a.m.
Royal Genovian Academy
Courtyard

Well, I'm definitely not on holiday any more.

When Rocky and I left for school this morning (we go in the same car now), there were so many reporters, news vans and tourists camped out in front of the palace, hoping to catch a glimpse of the many royals and celebrities who will be attending tomorrow's festivities, the Royal Genovian Guards had to come out mounted on horses to shoo them aside to open the gates!

Now there are apparently even *more* people and

news vans crowded around the palace than there were before, so the royal motorcade bringing Mia and Michael here to school to watch our performance of 'All Roads Lead to Genovia' is running late.

I don't know what it is about a royal wedding that makes people go so bananas.

And the ceremony is still twenty-four hours away!

I'm just sad that Nishi is missing all this. She wouldn't get out of bed this morning in time for the limo. Her mom says it's jet lag, but I think we might actually have overdone things a little on Nishi's first day in Genovia. Not only did we go *everywhere* in the palace, ride Chrissy, go swimming, talk for hours and eat about seven pounds of Genovian pastry *each*, but my sister and her friends ended up joining us by the pool for her 'bachelorette party', and it went on and on for hours . . . into the night-time, even. I could still hear them laughing and splashing when I went to bed, and that was long after Nishi fell fast asleep on her sun lounger without even having had any dinner. Nishi's mom had to ask Lars, Mia's bodyguard, to pick her up and carry her to her room because she was worried Nishi would catch a cold in her wet bathing suit. (Nishi's dad couldn't do it because he has back problems.)

My sister promised that if Nishi gets ready in time, she can come to school with Mia and Michael for the 'surprise'.

Actually, though, I'll be all right if Nishi doesn't come. Seeing all the people screaming excitedly outside the limo is one thing.

But seeing me in my national costume of Genovia is another. Maybe it's better if Nishi doesn't see that. It might be better if *no one* sees it. It might be better if Mia and Michael have to turn around and go back to the palace because the traffic is so terrible, and this whole performance gets cancelled!

I know that's a terrible thing to write or even feel, but I mean it: This is going to be a disaster!

Rocky and I kept our national costumes at school so the surprise wouldn't be spoilt, but now I'm kind of wondering if that was such a good idea, because I think if I had shown my dirndl to Francesca, my personal wardrobe consultant, she could have had it tailored to fit me better. It's much tighter than I remember it being when I first tried it on, and the puffy skirt is really itchy!

But a royal is never supposed to scratch in public.

I'm not the only one who is trying not to scratch. *All* of us girls are pretty miserable about it, especially since all we're doing is sitting here, waiting.

It's not fair, because the boys look really comfortable in their lederhosen . . . even Rocky, who threw the biggest fit about them! He looks like an elf. Everyone is saying so! Since it's the last day of school and also a special occasion and also because the motorcade is running late, Madame Alain has let us have our mobiles (only until 'the princess and her entourage' arrive and if we promise not to mess up our national costumes).

All the girls want to take selfies

with Rocky, even the high school girls. Queen Amina called him 'adorable' and lifted him up high into the air.

And Rocky doesn't even mind! I can tell because he hasn't mentioned farting or dinosaurs once (although this might be because he's shifted his full attention to iguanas now instead).

The only person who seemed to mind was Luisa.

'Disgusting. He isn't even royal!' I heard her mutter.

This made me mad, but I didn't say anything because I'm trying to be more understanding and tolerant of Luisa now that I know about her parents. If there's one thing I've learned since becoming a princess, it's that being gracious and kind to others who are less fortunate than you is important. And usually your kindness will be returned in the form of others being kind to you — like Prince Khalil helping with the iguana problem at the palace.

So maybe the mean, bossy snobs like Luisa will get the message and start trying to be more like the person I aspire to be.

Although I'm not sure how well this plan is working. Luisa doesn't even seem to have *noticed* how kind I am to everyone, let alone that I'm being kind to her.

And I think I might have been a little *too* kind to Prince Gunther. No matter how many times I tell him we're just friends, he still thinks there's a chance I might change my mind and visit him in Stockerdörfl.

'Lederhosen are what we normally wear there,' he told me while Victorine was making us pose together for a photo. 'For relaxation and for sport. That is why I am so relaxed in them. When you come to visit me this summer, Princess Olivia, you'll see.'

Uggghhhh!

Victorine thought this was very funny. She and Marguerite think Prince Gunther looks 'very hot' in his lederhosen.

Luisa says Prince Khalil looks hotter. I said it's not a contest. It's important for princesses to be diplomatic.

But I was lying. Of course Prince Khalil looks

hotter! Prince Khalil is definitely the cutest boy in the sixth grade. (Not that I like him. I'm only saying that from an artist's point of view, Prince Khalil is better looking than Prince Gunther. And of course Prince Khalil doesn't have green hair.)

So it would be very nice if Prince Gunther (and my cousin Luisa) would stop embarrassing me in front of him.

I still don't want to hurt Prince Gunther's feelings or anything, but there is no way I'm going to Stockerdörfl over the summer to visit him.

So in response to his invitation (the *third time* he's asked me), I said, 'I don't know, Prince Gunther. My sister is leaving for her honeymoon, and she asked me to take care of her cat, Fat Louie, while she's away. She's going to be gone for a very long time . . . two weeks.'

'Oh,' he said. 'Well, when she gets back, then—'

'Yes, but then she's going to have her formal coronation, accepting the throne from my dad. It's a whole big thing, and obviously I have to be here for *that*.'

'Of course,' he said. 'But then after that—'

'Well, after that, she's having twins, and I'm probably going to have to help her take care of them and run the country while she's on maternity leave and stuff. It might be very hard for me to get away. Maybe we can write instead.'

He looked kind of surprised, but in a good way.

'Write? Like letters? I love to write letters! I'm very good at writing letters. And texting. Maybe we can do both!'

So now I'm going to have to write letters (and texts) with Prince Gunther over summer break.

But I don't mind. It's better than going to visit him.

'Great,' I said. 'Well, goodbye.' I held out my hand.

'Goodbye?' He looked surprised again, but this time not in a good way. 'Why goodbye?'

'Because after the performance, I'm probably going to have to leave in a rush,' I said, 'to go home to start getting ready for my sister's wedding. So we should just say goodbye now.'

'Oh,' he said, and shook my hand. Fortunately, since I'd given him my lecture about being more careful with his flexing, he didn't crush my fingers into tiny sausages. 'Auf Wiedersehen, Your Highness.'

'Auf Wiedersehen,' I said.

PHEW. I'm glad that's over. Especially since the motorcade is here! Can't wait to get finished with this performance so I can:

- Go home and have mani-pedis with Nishi and my sister
- Be done with the Royal Genovian Academy for the whole summer
- Finally get out of this stupid costume
- Never sing 'All Roads Lead to Genovia' again
- Never, ever dance with Prince Gunther again
- Or even see him again until September

YAY!!!!!

Friday 19 June
2.30 p.m.
Royal Genovian Palace

Well, *that* did not go well.

Or I guess the problem is that it went *too* well.

Because my sister loved the RGA's performance of 'All Roads Lead to Genovia'.

She loved it so much that she's invited all the students (and teachers) at the RGA to her wedding reception, where she says she 'really, really hopes' we'll perform 'All Roads Lead to Genovia' again, because it is now her favourite song.

Madame Alain says this is a 'huge honour.'

Frankly, I don't agree.

Not that I don't think my sister really, really enjoyed our performance. I know she did. When I came up to her afterwards, she was crying because she was so moved.

'Oh no,' I cried. 'What's wrong?' I thought maybe she'd shut her finger in a door or something. The doors at the RGA are very old and heavy, just like the ones in the palace. It would be easy to smash your finger in one.

But that wasn't it at all. Mia grabbed and hugged me and said, 'That was the funniest — I mean, best — thing I've ever seen in my life! You guys were so, so good.'

And then I saw that she was laughing! So was Michael.

Both of them were laughing so hard that they *were crying*.

I don't know what about our performance made them laugh — 'All Roads Lead to Genovia' is quite a serious song. It isn't supposed to be funny.

But I guess it's good that they enjoyed it, especially since it was their wedding gift.

Only now I have to sing it — and dance it — again. And everyone I know at school is going to be at my house . . . just like Dad said was going to happen!

Including Gunther.

And I know it's a very big house (a palace, actually) with a lot of rooms in which I can hide from him if I have to. But I wasn't planning on having to hide from him at all, especially at my sister's wedding. I was planning on having a good time!

Even worse, Luisa pointed out just now that Gunther could ask me to dance with him.

'And not promenade Genovian-style, either, Olivia,' she teased, 'but slow dance in the moonlight in the royal gardens.'

'Ooooh,' Victorine and Marguerite said. Then they burst out laughing.

I really don't see what's so funny about any of this, even though I'm a Sagittarius and we're supposed to see the bright side of things.

But I guess I don't have a choice. We're in the

gardens right now, having aromatic salt rubs done on our hands and feet, and our finger- and toenails painted blush pink. Obviously, I wanted to get mine done bright yellow with purple sparkle polka dots, but we have to get what Paolo, the style consultant, says.

And he says we're all getting blush pink, so we'll match tomorrow on television.

We're each getting different hairstyles, though, with flower arrangements in our curls. 'Because every woman is unique,' Paolo says. 'Like the flower.'

I like this idea. I wonder what kind of flower I am. I think I'm a daisy. Daisies are cheerful but reliable.

I'm not saying anything to my sister about how inviting my entire school to her wedding may not have been the best idea (even though I don't think it was) because Mia is in the first really good mood I've seen her in all week, and I don't want to add to her stress.

I guess it's one thing to be called 'the World's

Prettiest Princess Bride' by RateTheRoyals.com, but it's quite another actually to have to *be* a princess bride and have people coming up to you going, 'Princess, we don't have a school for all the refugee children now that we have housing for them. What should we do?' and 'Princess, we don't have enough food for all the wedding guests. What should we do?'

When I went to grab Snowball out of the kitchens (I *knew* she was in there! Fortunately I caught her before anyone noticed . . . Now I'm keeping her on a leash next to my sun lounger), I overheard Chef Bernard freaking out.

'I just got the last shipment of spiny lobsters in all of southern Europe!' Chef Bernard was yelling. 'How am I going to stretch it out to feed *seven hundred* people? How? How?'

I know Mia thought she was doing a kind thing inviting everyone from the RGA to the reception, especially since we so touched her with our moving vocal and dance performance.

But not everyone is happy about it. Like Chef Bernard, for instance. Or me.

Oh well.

I guess that's not the point. Spreading joy throughout the land is. Prince Gunther is super happy about it. He's already texted me three times *while I've been writing this* to say how excited he is:

<HRH Prince Gunther   OlivGrace >

> Princess Olivia, when I see you tomorrow, I will have a surprise for you that I think you will like!

> Thanks, Gunther, that's really really really nice of you. But you don't need to do that.

> No, this I want to do, because you have been so kind to me.

Oh no! What could the surprise be?

I just showed this text to Nishi, and she went, 'Awwww! I want a prince to bring ME a surprise.'

'I know what it is,' Luisa said from her sun lounger. 'Skis!' Then she and Victorine and Marguerite laughed uproariously.

'Stop it, Luisa,' I said. 'It's not going to be skis.'

At least, I hope not.

'What are you girls laughing about?' my sister's friend Tina wanted to know.

'Nothing,' we all said in unison. Because it didn't seem very princessy to talk about boys in front of grown-ups.

'Oh,' she said. 'I thought it might be Boris P. Because you know he's going to be here any minute. Not that I care.'

It was awesome of her to say this, because it distracted Luisa and the other girls away from me and the Gunther situation. They all started squealing excitedly about Boris P, because it turns out he's a really big rock star, even in Genovia, where people are more interested in royalty than they are in rock stars, generally.

At least, people like Grandmère. I feel kind of bad that we didn't invite Prince Gunther's parents to the wedding.

But he said (in another text that I just got! Number four!) that they couldn't have come, due to being at a yoga retreat in India. He was going to have had to stay at school all weekend anyway because his parents weren't coming to pick him up until Monday, partly due to not being home and partly due to having heard the traffic in and around Genovia tomorrow was going to be so bad, thanks to the wedding. They've already issued warnings up and down the coast about it!

Poor Gunther!

But when I mentioned this to Grandmère just now (about the traffic warnings), she got *excited* instead of concerned. She started bragging to everyone who would listen, gesturing so violently with her hands that Rommel, who was sitting on her lap as she got her toenails done, almost fell off.

'Traffic jams along the coast,' she cried to Michael's mom, Dr Moscovitz, who was sitting on the sun lounger next to her. 'Did you hear? Traffic jams along the coast!'

'Oh,' Dr Moscovitz said, looking bewildered. 'Is that a good thing?'

'Of course it is!' Grandmère shouted. 'It's a

tremendous thing! It's a spectacular thing! More traffic means more tourist dollars for Genovia! This wedding is going to save this country from financial ruin!'

'Oh,' Dr Moscovitz said, smiling. 'How lovely. I'm delighted my son could help.'

I'm glad Grandmère is in such a good mood.

And things are only getting better, since Sebastiano really liked her idea about dyeing all the bridesmaid dresses purple. He just came over to the side of the pool and said, 'Look at all these beaut

ladies! You are look like the mermaids by the crystal grotto!' (My cousin Sebastiano, the fashion designer, speaks about as much English as I speak Italian, and often remembers only the first syllable of words.)

Luisa and Victorine and Marguerite and Nishi and Mia's friends asked Sebastiano if their dresses were ready, and he said, '*Si*' (*Si* is *yes* in Italian). 'They are ready, and are even more beaut than you will remem!'

Then I saw him wink at Grandmèrc, who only smiled mysteriously (a royal never winks).

Which must mean the dye worked!

Everyone is going to be so surprised . . . especially Mia.

But surprised in a good way, hopefully, like she was with the 'All Roads Lead to Genovia' performance.

I just wish I could figure out what to give Mia and Michael as a wedding present. Because I really don't think a dance in dirndls makes a good present for anyone.

Friday 19 June
4.00 p.m.
Royal Throne Room
Wedding Rehearsal

I cannot believe my cousin Luisa.

Seriously. I cannot *believe someone like her actually exists*!

I know it's not completely her fault because she has an unhappy home life (at least according to Princess Komiko and Grandmère, too, if everything she's said about Luisa's grandmother the baroness is true).

But that doesn't give her an excuse to act like a complete brat!

Everything was going fine — we were getting along pretty well at the pool — until it was time to get dressed and go to the wedding rehearsal.

It wasn't a *dress* rehearsal, so no one has seen their bridesmaid dresses yet (thank goodness, because we don't need any MORE drama, which is apparently what Luisa specializes in).

But it was the first time we'd seen the boys since the performance this morning.

Well, one boy in particular. You can guess which one.

OK. Prince Khalil.

For some reason, when the boys were around — Michael and my dad and Rocky and the rest of the groomsmen, meaning you-know-who . . . PRINCE KHALIL — *some* of the girls in the wedding party began to act a little bit silly, doing the Whip and Nae Nae down the aisle instead of walking with proper grace and decorum, like Vivianne, the director of Palace Affairs, instructed us.

OK, ONE girl in the wedding party started doing this: Lady Luisa Ferrari.

She wouldn't take anything that Vivianne was saying seriously! She kept goofing about, especially any time she had to walk in front of me and Nishi, which was basically *all the time*!!

The way the royal wedding worked was, the boys walked down the aisle first, after the prime minister, who's the person who'll be marrying Mia and Michael tomorrow. So, first the groomsmen and Michael, then Rocky with the rings (for the rehearsal they were using fake ones, thank goodness, so there was less chance of his losing them).

Then the bridesmaids went.

Then the junior bridesmaids, Victorine, Marguerite and Luisa.

Luisa and Victorine and Marguerite were supposed to scatter flower petals on the red carpet in front of my sister (white flower petals, not purple ones. Grandmère and I agreed that white flower petals would look better on the red carpet than purple ones).

Then Mia, escorted by her mom and dad (in Genovia, it's traditional for both of the bride's parents to give her away), walked down the long aisle, followed by me and Nishi, holding the fifteen-foot train to Mia's bridal gown.

Only for rehearsal, Mia was wearing a fifteen-foot tablecloth as her train (because it's bad luck for the groom to see the bride in her wedding gown before the big day) so that Nishi and I could get a feel for it . . . and so that the television people could figure out where to put their lights and cameras and everything.

So it was super annoying that Luisa was goofing about as much as she was, since some of us had serious practising to do (and also because her goofing about kept making Victorine and Marguerite laugh, and then they weren't concentrating, either).

Also, I personally don't think it impressed Prince Khalil at all! He didn't even seem to notice. He was standing up at the front of the throne room with Michael and Boris P and the rest of the groomsmen, showing photos on his mobile to Rocky. Probably photos of snakes and amphibians, based on Rocky's excited expression.

Of course, I *understand* why Luisa was trying so hard to get his attention. When she saw Prince Khalil, Nishi dug her nails into me and said, 'OMG, Olivia! He's sooooo cute! Why didn't you TELL me?'

But still! No matter how cute Prince Khalil might be, Luisa was trying get his attention in the *wrong way*. It wasn't very royal of her to waste everyone's time, especially during a wedding rehearsal, when we all wanted to be somewhere else (like the pool), or, in the case of the prime minister, actually had somewhere important to be, such as her job.

Finally Grandmère had to say, in a voice so cold that it echoed through the throne room, 'Luisa Ferrari. Perhaps you would prefer to attend this wedding as a guest rather than a junior bridesmaid.'

Only then did Luisa stop acting so full of herself. 'Pardon me, Your Majesty,' she said, and curtsied. Ha!

Only instead of admitting she'd been in the wrong, Luisa came running over to me while we were sitting in the hallway while the TV people were working on the lighting, and whispered, 'Kee-yow, Olivia! What is that bony old lady's problem? Of course I'll do it properly tomorrow. But unlike SOME people, I don't need to rehearse WALKING. I've been doing fashion shows since I was a child. My mother signed me up with the top modelling agency in Genovia when I was a baby.'

I glared at her. 'Don't say "kee-yow" to me. And if my grandmother hears you call her a bony old lady, she'll throw you in the dungeon.'

Luisa rolled her eyes. 'Oh please. There isn't even a dungeon in this palace any more. I heard your father converted it into a wine cellar.'

Sadly, this is true.

It was right then that IT happened. The thing that gave Luisa a COMPLETE ROYAL WEDDING BREAKDOWN. There's no other way to describe it.

'Hi, Olivia,' Prince Khalil walked over to say. 'I don't think I've had a chance to meet your friend yet.'

Nishi's eyes grew about five sizes larger than

usual. Before I could say anything, she scrambled to her feet and curtsied. 'H-h-hello, Your Royal Highness,' she said to Prince Khalil. 'I'm Nishi Desai. I'm Olivia's friend from New Jersey.'

'Hi, Nishi from New Jersey,' Prince Khalil said with a grin. He didn't seem to notice that Luisa's face had turned bright red with rage. 'It's a pleasure to meet you. So, Princess Olivia,' he said, turning back to me, 'I wanted to tell you, we'll try to have all of the cages out by tonight. But we haven't caught all of your iguanas. There are always a few left over that are too smart for the live traps. Plus there will be nests with eggs in them. We'll have to tackle those next week.'

'Oh,' I said. 'Sure. OK. Thanks.'

'Great!' He smiled at me, and I couldn't help noticing again how nice his eyes looked when he smiled. What is wrong with me? 'Well, see you down the aisle.'

That was a little joke, because we kept having to walk down the aisle over and over again for rehearsal. Though not together, of course.

'Ha,' I said. 'See you down the aisle.'

As soon as he went back into the throne room, Nishi squealed and squeezed my arm and jumped up and down a few times.

'Oh my gosh!' she gushed. 'A real prince! I finally met a real prince! I mean, besides your dad. And he's soooo cute!'

But I hardly noticed, because Luisa was giving me a death stare. Seriously. She looked like she was going to kill me.

'What,' Luisa demanded, 'was *that* all about?'

I should have said, 'None of your business, Luisa,' because I have a perfect right to talk to anyone I want to without her permission.

But since I'm a princess and have compassion for others, and I know how big a crush she has on him, I said, 'Luisa, Khalil is a member of the Genovian Herpetology Rescue Society, and they've been helping to remove unwanted iguanas from the palace gardens before everyone gets here for the wedding. So relax. It's not as if he likes me or anything.'

But I guess this was the wrong thing to say,

because instead of taking my advice and relaxing, Luisa got even more mad. Her nostrils pinched together and she said, '*You*? Why would someone like *him* ever like someone like *you*? Trust me, *that* thought never even entered my mind!'

That hurt my feelings a little bit . . . and reminded me of the mean drawing she'd made and left on my desk. Maybe that hadn't really been a joke meant to 'help' me after all. Maybe that had been how my cousin Luisa really sees me.

'What do you mean, someone like me?' I asked, putting my hands on my hips. 'What's wrong with me?'

'What *isn't* wrong with you?' Luisa shot back. 'You're the worst excuse for a princess I ever saw. You wear glasses, your hair is a curly mess, you can't speak proper Italian . . . and you *certainly* can't dance. You looked completely absurd at the performance today.'

I heard Nishi gasp. 'That isn't true! Olivia is an amazing dancer! And I love her hair.'

I saw Victorine and Marguerite exchange glances. 'Yeah, Luisa,' Marguerite said. 'I think you're being a little harsh. Just because Olivia and Prince Khalil are friends—'

But even though Marguerite was trying to exercise a little royal diplomacy, this turned out to be the worst thing she could have said.

'Oh, Olivia and Prince Khalil are "friends" now?' Luisa snapped. 'Just how "friendly" are you with Prince Khalil, Olivia?'

'What?' I had no idea what she was talking about, but Marguerite and Victorine seemed to, since they exchanged meaningful looks, their eyebrows raised. 'Luisa, I told you. He only came over here a few times to help get rid of our iguanas.'

'If all he did while he was here was get rid of your iguanas, *Princess* Olivia, then how come you never told me about it?' Luisa demanded. 'Why was it such a secret?'

'It . . . it wasn't a secret,' I stammered. 'I mean, it was a secret from my sister, because it was supposed to be a wedding surprise for her, like the presentation. But it wasn't a secret from you.'

'Then why didn't you tell me?' Luisa yelled. Fortunately the only people who were around were Nishi and my cousins and a few palace staff members, not Prince Khalil or the prime minister or anyone else in the bridal party, since they were all still inside the throne room. Otherwise I'd have been even more mortified. 'You know I like him!'

'Um,' Nishi said. 'Not to interrupt, but Olivia told me she IS just friends with Prince Khalil. If that helps.'

'Well, it doesn't,' Luisa said, and flipped some of her long blond hair. 'Thank you very much. And it might interest you to know, Nisha, or whatever your name is, that your friend is a boyfriend stealer.'

I gasped. So did Victorine and Marguerite. So did Nishi. So did some of the palace staff members.

'No,' I said, feeling my eyes fill with tears. 'I'm not. I'm really not!'

'Kee-yow, Olivia,' Luisa said. 'Was I ever wrong about you. I thought you and I were going to be friends. But I can see now that you're just another royal backstabber. Well, look out, because two can play at that game.'

Friday 19 June
6.30 p.m.
Royal Genovian Bedroom

Nishi says I should just ignore Luisa. 'She's obviously demented.'

'Maybe,' I said. 'But she's still my cousin.'

'So what? I have a lot of cousins, too,' Nishi pointed out. 'One of them holds the record for owning the world's largest rubber-band ball. That doesn't mean I'd ever take anything he said seriously, because he's as crazy as Luisa is.'

'Good point.'

Still, I can't help feeling terrible about what Luisa

called me — a royal backstabber and a boyfriend stealer. Even if I didn't do what she accused me of doing, I don't want anyone to think badly of me . . . even a snob like Luisa.

I felt so horrible about the whole thing that when we were all getting ready for dinner, I went down the hall from my room to Grandmère's, hoping I could ask her advice about what I should do. I've had good luck following Grandmère's advice in the past. And I knew everyone else would be busy with pre-wedding jitters.

Grandmère doesn't get the jitters.

Her maid answered the door, and, seeing it was me, let me in. Grandmère issued a rule that I'm always allowed into her room unless she has other company.

Just like I thought, no jitters. Grandmère was still in her robe and turban, applying a thick white cream to her hands and neck. Grandmère says a lady should moisturize regularly, or she'll live to regret it.

'Olivia,' she said, 'why aren't you getting ready for dinner? Don't tell me you're feeling nervous about the ceremony tomorrow. It's only live television. If you make a fool of yourself, someone else will soon do something even more foolish, and everyone will quickly forget all about you.'

'Thanks, Grandmère,' I said. 'No, I'm not worried about tomorrow. Or at least I wasn't until you said that. Now I am. But I'm more worried about Luisa Ferrari.'

'Luisa Ferrari?' Grandmère put down her cold cream and widened her eyes. 'What about her?'

So I told her all about Luisa . . . how she always said 'kee-yow' to me, and how she was in love with Prince Khalil and thought I was in love with him, too (which I told Grandmère I am definitely NOT . . . although I do like the way Prince Khalil loves iguanas, and wants to save them all, and is always reading books about them, and how curly his hair is, and how his dark brown eyes look when he smiles).

And how even though I did NOT in any way steal Prince Khalil from her, Luisa thinks I'm a back-stabber, and that she may or not be thinking of doing something nasty to get back at me over it.

'I'm not saying any of this because I want to get Luisa in trouble,' I said when I was done. 'I know a royal never tattles. I just think someone should know. An adult. Just in case.'

Grandmère nodded, picked up a different jar, and began rubbing a new cream on to her face. She always says a woman should avoid three things: the sun, tanning beds, and men standing on the street selling perfume.

'Of course. I understand perfectly, and you did the right thing telling me, Olivia. None of this, of course, has anything to do with you. It's Bianca Ferrari's fault.'

'It is?' I was surprised. 'How?'

'Bianca Ferrari is probably filling her granddaughter's head with tales of how SHE should be the rightful heir to the throne, not you. Luisa's grandmother thought *she* would marry your grandfather some day, you see,' she said, examining her reflection in the mirror. 'Oh, I suppose your grandfather was fond of her, in his way . . . until I came along. Then he realized what a real woman was and never looked in Bianca Ferrari's direction again.'

I gasped. 'Grandmère! *You* were a boyfriend stealer? A royal backstabber?'

'Pfuit!' She picked up a lipstick and began carefully to apply it. 'You can't steal what someone never owned in the first place. Bianca Ferrari always had beauty, but not character or common sense. And those are the things one ought to look for in a life partner, because beauty fades, but character and common sense are forever.'

'Oh,' I said.

'Yes, Olivia, *oh*. That is why your cousin is filled with so much hostility towards you. Because you have both character *and* common sense, which Luisa, for now, seems to lack. That — in addition to the fact that you're a princess, while she's only the grand-daughter of a baroness — makes her feel insecure.'

I wasn't so sure about that. Luisa Ferrari seemed like the least insecure person I'd ever met.

But Grandmère went on, 'Character and common sense can be learned, of course. That's what a good education is for. But right now Luisa appears to prefer to spend her time focusing on her looks, and on securing a royal title for herself, perhaps in the form of marrying a prince.' She looked at my reflection in the mirror and smiled. 'But she's young. There's still plenty of time for her to learn. And as royals ourselves, it's our duty to help guide her, Olivia, into making the right choices.'

I had no idea what she was talking about. I wanted to spend as little time as possible with Luisa. But if it was for the good of the throne — and the family — I guess I'd try to help. 'How, Grandmère?'

'I think both Luisa and her grandmother could learn to be a little more tolerant of others,' Grandmère said. 'Especially commoners. It would be character-building for them. But the only way that's going to happen is if they spend more time with them.'

I thought of what Luisa had said about Rocky not being 'royal' and how he shouldn't even be attending the RGA.

'Um,' I said. 'I guess. But I don't see how that will ever—'

'Leave it to me,' Grandmère interrupted briskly, and removed her turban to reveal a perfectly coiffed bun. 'Maxine, my tiara, please.'

'Yes, Your Highness.' Maxine, Grandmère's maid, went to Grandmère's jewel closet to fetch her tiara.

'Olivia, you had better go to your own room and get your own tiara. This is a formal dinner tonight. Hats and bats, my girl. Hats and bats.'

Hats and bats is code in the palace for 'tiara and sceptre'.

'Yes, Grandmère,' I said, and went back to my room, thinking about everything she'd said. I don't know if I believe Luisa Ferrari is jealous of my character and common sense . . . and my royal title, of course. I think Princess Komiko is right, and Luisa is mean because her parents don't get along and she's mad about it and thinks it's OK to take that anger out on other people.

Maybe we're both right. Like I told Prince Khalil, people can be more than one thing. Human beings are complicated.

But in the end, it doesn't really matter, because no matter why Luisa is the way she is, I'm the one who has to deal with it.

Friday 19 June
8.30 p.m.
Royal Banquet Hall
Prenuptial Dinner

I know I'm not supposed to be writing in my notebook at the table, but I have to because I'm SURE Luisa is up to something. All night long she's been giving me dirty looks from across the dining room!

Then again, that might be because I'm sitting next to Michael's mom, Dr Moscovitz, who really is very nice and funny, while Luisa has to sit by some old boring friend that her grandmother invited who won't stop talking about the stock market.

HA HA HA HA!

Oops, I know it's wrong to gloat over the misfortune of others.

But it's hard not to be having fun at your sister's prenuptial dinner, where everyone is toasting the bride and groom and telling funny stories about how they first kissed in a penguin enclosure at the zoo (Nishi thinks this is very romantic) and went to something called a Cultural Diversity Dance and how Michael used to be in a band.

Even Rocky seems to be having fun, and he hates big formal dinners like this (but he gets to sit next to Prince Khalil, so basically, Rocky is in heaven).

I never noticed before — maybe because I've never seen him in a tuxedo — but Prince Khalil looks a lot like one of those Bollywood movie stars that Nishi is always going on about, the ones who can sing and dance at the same time, unlike me.

And he's being *so nice* to Rocky! Some boys aren't nice to other boys who are younger than they are. Sometimes they ignore them or even bully them (my step-cousin Justin used to).

But Khalil is being very patient and kind to Rocky, even showing him which spoon to use for the soup, and making sure he knows which water glass to drink out of, so he doesn't make the same mistake I did the other night.

Awwww!

Not that I like him or anything. I —

Ugh! There's Luisa, giving me the death stare AGAIN! What is her *problem*? I should probably tell someone besides Grandmère what's going on . . . someone like Lars, Mia's bodyguard, the head of the Royal Genovian Guard.

But no, that might be overreacting a little. Probably Grandmère is right, and Luisa only needs our guidance and example as royals. My job as a junior bridesmaid (and princess) is to help my sister AVOID trouble during her wedding, not MAKE it for her.

And I'm sure Grandmère's plan (whatever it is) is going to work.

So I'm going to keep my mouth shut. I mean,

really, Luisa is a bridesmaid, too. The wedding is when she's going to have her big opportunity to show off her Claudio evening gown with the detachable skirt in front of everyone. What is she going to do, try to ruin it? Of course not!

Friday 19 June
11.45 p.m.
Royal Genovian Bedroom

I went to bed early (or tried to, anyway) because Grandmère said we should all get our beauty sleep or every line on our faces would show up tomorrow on people's televisions while we were being filmed at the wedding (at least on the high-definition TVs).

But just after I fell asleep, I had the worst, most terrible nightmare. I was in my purple bridesmaid dress (and I looked really, really amazing in it), and the wedding was about to start, but all of a sudden I couldn't find Snowball!

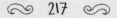

And this was bad because for some reason she was supposed to walk down the aisle with me (in the dream. In real life, pets aren't allowed to be in the wedding, which I think is terrible and so does Mia. For a while she was saying it would be funny if Fat Louie could ride down the aisle on the back of her train, until Sebastiano pointed out that this would ruin her veil because it's made of hand-stitched lace and it would tear apart if a twenty-pound cat sat on it and got dragged down a red carpet. Not to mention, Fat Louie would never sit still for it).

So in my dream I was running all around the palace, looking everywhere for Snowball, calling, 'Snowball! Snowy! Here, Snowball, come here, girl! Where are you, girl?'

And then when I finally found her in Chrissy's stable, I was so relieved . . .

Until the worst thing happened! She came running up to me and jumped up excitedly (which I've been trying to train her not to do), and got dirty paw marks all over my beautiful purple bridesmaid dress!

It was horrible! I looked like a total mess!

But there was no time to clean off the paw marks (and they wouldn't have come out anyway, because they were *everywhere*), since it was time to walk down the aisle, and Mia was calling me.

So I had to hold my sister's bridal train with *dirty paw marks all over me.*

And everyone was staring and whispering about me and what a failure I was as a princess, in spite of all the training that Mia and Dad and Grandmère and the RGA and everyone had given me, and how I'd ruined the WHOLE WEDDING.

And then the dream shifted to a news report of a traffic jam due to all the people who were *leaving* Genovia, vowing never to come back because of me!

Fortunately that's when I woke up.

I was so relieved to find Snowball curled up next to me asleep in a little ball, without the slightest hint of dirt on her, that I grabbed and hugged her.

And now I'm going to make sure she stays locked in my room ALL NIGHT and ALL MORNING if it's the last thing I do!

I won't be the one to ruin this wedding. I WON'T!

Saturday 20 June
7.45 a.m.
Royal Genovian Bedroom
Wedding Day

I hate her.

I. Hate. Her.

I know it's wrong to say you hate people, but I don't care.

I HATE LUISA FERRARI.

She is all the worst things in the world combined, every bad swear word I have ever heard my dad call the contractors who are working on the summer house, AND a bad person, besides.

And I KNOW it was her, because Snowball was

with me ALL NIGHT! I made sure because of my nightmare.

So Snowball couldn't have snuck down to the kitchen in the middle of the night and stolen the top layer off the wedding cake and eaten it!

How would Snowball even have REACHED the top layer of the wedding cake without knocking the whole thing down, anyway? The wedding cake is five feet tall (and on a table with no chairs around it).

OBVIOUSLY a human being had to have done it. You don't have to be a member of the Royal Genovian Guard, trained in the art of investigation and mystery detection, to deduce that.

But the majordomo doesn't believe me. Neither does Chef Bernard. When he and the rest of the cooking staff came in this morning and saw what had happened to the cake, of course they all assumed it was Snowball. I don't really blame them, because of her previous crimes.

Still, she couldn't possibly have done this! Somehow last night Luisa had to have snuck into the kitchen and done it, in order to ruin my life. It's almost like my dream is coming true, in a way. I wonder if I'm a little bit psychic? Is it possible to be a princess, good at drawing, and *also* psychic?

No. That's too many good things at once.

'Look,' I said to them as calmly as I could, using as many of my diplomacy skills as I could muster, because I knew I couldn't outright blame Luisa without having any proof. 'It couldn't possibly have been Snowball. Snowball was with me all night. And she isn't tall enough to have reached the top of that cake without leaving paw prints on the rest of it. Unless you think she FLEW to the top.'

Everyone looked at the cake. It was only me, Dad and Grandmère there from the family, because they didn't want to disturb anyone else in the palace (like Mia) because it was 'only a domestic issue', and also because Mia was the bride and 'needed her rest'.

Only a domestic issue? My dog was being accused of a crime she didn't commit!

'Olivia has a point,' Dad said. 'It would have taken a feat of true engineering.'

'But how else could it have happened?' the

majordomo wailed. 'Who would take the top layer — only the top layer — of a seven-layer wedding cake? We have searched everywhere, but it is gone.'

'That's more proof that it wasn't Snowball,' I said. 'Because if it was her, you'd have found bits of cake lying around somewhere. Snowball never eats *everything* she steals. She always hides some for later. So if it was Snowball, there would be icing and crumbs somewhere on the grounds of this palace.'

My dad looked unhappy. He was wearing his robe, which is red satin and has a fancy letter *P*, either for Prince or Phillipe, on the lapel.

'I don't want to have the grounds searched for the top layer of a royal wedding cake right now,' he said. 'The guests are going to be arriving in a few hours.'

'Why don't we all go back to bed,' Grandmère said, putting an arm around my shoulders. 'I think Chef Bernard has the situation well in hand.'

'*Non!*' Chef Bernard cried. '*Non*, I do not! This cake was to have served five hundred and fifty. Now it is to serve seven hundred, thanks to zee children from the zee school. But it is MISSING A LAYER!'

Grandmère blinked at him. 'Oh, for heaven's sake, Chef. Just cut smaller slices.'

Both Chef Bernard and the majordomo looked like they wanted to cut something — and not a slice of cake, either.

'Yes, Your Highness,' the chef said sadly.

As we were walking back up the stairs to our bedrooms, I said to Dad, feeling desperate, 'Snowball didn't do it. You *have* to see that.'

'Of course I do, sweetheart,' Dad said, yawning.

'Not a word about any of this to anyone, you two,' Grandmère said. 'I don't want Amelia to know about *anything* that goes wrong today. Not that anything else is going to go wrong. The sun is shining, the crowds are already ten-deep outside . . . it looks like a fine day for a wedding. It's a pity about the cake, but . . . well, these things do happen.'

Dad rubbed his bald head. 'I don't see how. I've never seen anything like it. Do you suppose it *could* have been the dog?'

'NO!' I yelled. 'It wasn't. It was—'

But Grandmère gave me her most evil stare.

'Nothing else is going to go wrong today,' Grandmère said firmly. '*Nothing*. Do you understand, Olivia?'

I swallowed. 'Yes, Grandmère.'

It's not fair! Why should I have to act like a princess, when Luisa Ferrari gets to do whatever she wants, and get away with it? I don't care how sad she was when her parents got divorced, or how lacking she might be in character or common sense.

The next time I see Luisa Ferrari, she's going to get what she deserves.

Saturday 20 June
9.35 a.m.
Royal Genovian Bedroom
Wedding Day

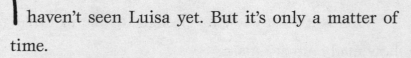

I haven't seen Luisa yet. But it's only a matter of time.

Right now Nishi and I are both getting our hair done by Paolo.

Well, by his assistants. Paolo — Hair Stylist to Royalty — only has time for one person today, and that's my sister, the bride.

The florists sent over arrangements for our hair — which Paolo's assistants are tucking in along with my tiara — as well as bouquets for us to hold.

In order to look good for the camera, we're also getting make-up. Not a lot, because it's important to appear 'natural and dewy fresh' like the young girls that we are (according to orders given by Dominique de Bois, director of Royal Genovian Press Relations and Marketing).

But when you're being filmed in high definition, that means being sprayed with a light film of foundation that exactly matches your own skin colour, so there won't be any uneven spots (the lady doing my make-up told me that even male sports stars do this).

This is almost exciting enough for me to forget how mad I am at Luisa.

Almost.

Nishi says she is in paradise (although we both agreed we're glad we don't have to get sprayed every day).

After the make-up and hair comes the next most important part:

THE DRESSES!

Ours were delivered, newly pressed, by the housekeeping staff in garment bags, so I couldn't see what mine looked like until Francesca, my personal wardrobe consultant, unzipped it. When she did, she paused before taking it out of the bag.

'Oh my,' she said. 'Your Highness, I don't know how to tell you this, but your dress, it . . . it's . . . purple.'

'Surprise!' I cried.

'I LOVE it!' Nishi yelled when she saw hers.

'I know,' I said. 'Grandmère and I had Sebastiano dye them at the last minute. We think Mia will be so surprised.'

'Yes,' said Francesca, helping me to step into all the flouncy layers. 'I think the princess will be very surprised indeed.'

I hope it will be a good surprise! I think I look as good as I did in my dream . . . only better, because I'm not covered in dirty paw prints. Snowball is sitting on my bed, watching us, perfectly dirt-free (when I took her out for her morning walk, I was careful to keep her on her leash, and away from all puddles).

After all the hair and make-up people went away,

Nishi and I checked out our reflections in the full-length mirror in my bathroom.

'We look like naiads,' Nishi said approvingly. 'Those were a type of water nymph that lived in fountains and streams and stuff in ancient Greece. We look just like them, only in purple instead of green or blue.'

'Cool,' I said. 'Total naiads.'

Then we took a bunch of selfies with Nishi's mobile, posing on my bed that's shaped like a boat, so we looked even more like naiads, or maybe even the mermaid spigots on Grandmère's royal bathtub.

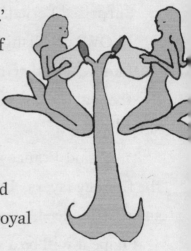

Now Francesca has left to go and see when they're going to be ready for us to come down, and Nishi is coming up with plans to get revenge on Luisa (because of course I told Nishi what Luisa did, even though Grandmère said not to. But Nishi won't tell Mia).

Nishi and Olivia's Plans to Get Revenge on Luisa Ferrari

Nishi Plan #1:

Trip Luisa in front of television cameras so her skirt falls over her head and her underwear shows in front of worldwide audience.

Olivia's note:

No. Luisa would like this as she craves attention. Also, it might ruin Mia's wedding and I promised Grandmère I wouldn't let anything happen to ruin Mia's day.

Nishi Plan #2:

Trip Luisa in front of wedding carriage. Luisa gets run over.

Olivia's note:

Luisa might be seriously hurt from this and we could go to jail. Jail is not very princessy. Also, remember my promise to Grandmère.

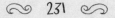

Nishi Plan #3:

Get Luisa alone. Get her to confess what she did. Record confession on mobile. Upload video to Internet so everyone sees it.

Olivia's note:

Better! But I still think this might give Luisa the attention she wants. She could become an international Internet sensation, and then write a bestselling book about it.

Nishi Plan #4:

Buy poison. Poison her.

Olivia's note:

Like I said, jail is not very princessy. Also, where do we buy poison? And having one of the junior bridesmaids die of poisoning would COMPLETELY ruin Mia's wedding.

Nishi Plan #5:

Get some of Chrissy's horse poo. Put poo in wedding cake. Give cake to Luisa.

Olivia's note:

Won't Luisa smell the horse poo? Also, I don't
want to touch horse poo. That's gross! Also, I'm
pretty sure she get could really sick from this,
and then we'd have to go to jail. Plus maybe
then all the other wedding guests will think there
is poo in the wedding cake, and this will ruin the
wedding.

Nishi Plan #6:
Ask Boris P to call Luisa up to the stage and
dedicate a song just to her. While she is onstage
staring up at him, all googly-eyed, have him change the
song so it is about how horrible she is.

Olivia's note:

But this might make Luisa feel so bad, it will
ruin her self-esteem, and then she will never develop
character or common sense. Royals are supposed to
guide those less fortunate, not destroy them.

Nishi Plan #6, continued:
Call Prince Khalil to come over and see Boris P

singing the song about how horrible Luisa is. Then he will know the truth about her, and then Prince Khalil will like you and not Luisa!

This is when I had to tell Nishi that I didn't want to play this game any more. It wasn't fun and also seemed mean. Also, that I don't like Prince Khalil.

But Nishi wouldn't listen! She had the nerve to say, 'I think you *do* like Prince Khalil, and I think he likes you back. I think Luisa knows that, and that's why she wrecked your sister's cake.'

My heart started beating kind of quickly when she said that. I don't know why. I said, 'Nishi, no. That's not true.'

'It is true. Anyone can see it. Even Rocky. Here, I'll go get Rocky and ask him.'

'No,' I said. 'Why would you get Rocky? He's just a little boy who doesn't know anything. Leave him out of this.'

But Nishi said, 'I'm getting him anyway. I'm going to ask him about the poo.'

'Nishi, no!' I said. 'I thought you were joking about the poo! Let's just drop it. Be serious now. The wedding is going to start soon. We need to—'

But she left before I could stop her. She flounced right out of my room (it's hard not to flounce in these dresses; they have so many petticoats) and down the hall.

What choice did I have? I had to follow her. I didn't want her busting in on Rocky and telling him about the poo (especially seeing as how it was so stupid. Although knowing Rocky, he might take it seriously) and getting him all riled up before the wedding.

That's how I know the truth now — the truth about Rocky. It's all Nishi's fault.

It wasn't Luisa who stole the top layer of Mia's wedding cake.

It wasn't Snowball, either.

It was Rocky.

Saturday 20 June
10.05 a.m.
Rocky's Room
Wedding Day

'I don't know what made me do it!' That's what Rocky keeps saying. 'I saw it there, and it just looked so delicious!'

I *bet* it was delicious. My sister and Michael have good taste. And the cake they picked out — chocolate cake with vanilla frosting — is the best kind.

Chocolate cake with vanilla frosting is *all over* the inside of Rocky's rocket ship to the moon. Also, little white Genovian frosting roses and tiny sparkly frosting snowflakes, which had decorated the top of Mia and Michael's cake.

At least until someone stole it.

Someone who was *not* my dog, Snowball, *or* my cousin Luisa Ferrari.

'Oh, Rocky,' I said, looking at the mess inside his cardboard rocket ship. 'How *could* you?'

'I don't know. I went down to the kitchen for a midnight snack and no one was there and I saw it and I thought — well, the cake was so big! I didn't think anyone would notice one little layer. Especially the top. It was so little.'

'The top's the most important part!' I cried. 'That's where they put the most decorations!'

'They take the top off and save it to eat a year later, for good luck,' Nishi said.

'Well,' he said, shrugging, 'I saved them the trouble by eating it.' Then he looked sad. 'But I guess it wasn't very good luck for me. Are . . . are you going to tell?'

'Everyone thinks it was Olivia's dog!' Nishi cried. 'Well, except for us. We thought it was Luisa Ferrari.

We came in here to ask you to throw some of Chrissy's poo at her.'

Rocky brightened. 'I still will, if you want me to.'

'NO!' I didn't know what to do. I was mad, but more at myself than at Rocky. I couldn't believe I'd been so quick to blame a girl — my cousin, a fellow classmate, who may not be the nicest person, but is technically only a little insecure — for something a nine-year-old boy had done. 'And no, we're not going to tell on you.'

He looked relieved. 'Phew! Thanks. I owe you one, Liv.'

'Yes,' I said. 'You do. And we're going to have to throw out your rocket ship now, you know, Rocky. We can't leave it like this; the cardboard is too messy. It will grow mould, and mice might get into it.' People don't know this, but even thousand-year-old palaces get mice. Maybe even *more* than other, newer palaces.

Rocky sighed. 'That's all right. I think . . . I think I might be ready to give up my rocket ship.'

I looked at him in astonishment. 'You *are*?' I asked. 'Since when?'

'Since yesterday,' he said. 'I don't want to go to the moon any more to visit the dinosaurs. I want to stay here in Genovia and study reptiles. And amphibians.'

Nishi started laughing. 'You and everybody else around here!'

I glared at her. I didn't see what was so funny. 'I think the study of reptiles and amphibians is very noble.'

'Ha,' Nishi laughed. 'You would!'

I still didn't see what was so funny, but I didn't get a chance to ask, because just then the door to Rocky's room opened, and Francesca peeked in. 'Oh, there you are, Your Highness,' she said. 'I've been looking everywhere for you. It's time.'

!!!!!

Saturday 20 June
Noon
Royal Throne Room
Wedding Day

It's happening. It's finally happening!

My sister looks beautiful. Her dress is perfect. When she came down the stairs, the light from the windows caught the tiny crystals sewn on to the bodice and the entwined letter Ms on the skirt of her gown — M for Mia, and M for Michael — and blazed like diamonds! She's always looked like a princess to me, but at that moment, she looked like a QUEEN.

Even my dad and Grandmère were stunned into silence for a moment as they watched her come down the stairs, and I noticed that Mia's mom was crying. Everyone was crying a little, I think, even the majordomo and Chef Bernard, who snuck upstairs from the kitchen to catch a glimpse of the bride as she made her way to the throne room.

But they were crying in a happy way.

'Well?' Mia said when she got to the bottom of the staircase. 'Isn't someone going to say something?'

'You look hot, P.O.G.,' said Michael's sister, Lilly, breaking the silence.

P.O.G. stands for Princess of Genovia. Everyone laughed except Michael, who wasn't there because he wasn't allowed to see the bride until she walked down the aisle. He and the groomsmen were already in the throne room with the prime minister.

It was right then that Rocky did something terrible . . . or wonderful, depending. He stepped up to his sister, his hand on his sword hilt (some not-very-intelligent person had decided it would be a good idea for Rocky to wear a tiny formal Genovian military uniform to the wedding, so he could match his soon-to-be adoptive dad), and said, 'Mia, I'm the one who stole the top of your cake.'

Mia looked down at him, her tiara sparkling wildly, and said, 'Excuse me?'

'I did it,' Rocky said. 'It was me. I'm sorry. I ate it. Don't worry, though, everyone is going to love it. It tasted delici—'

'Ooooh-kay,' Dad said, lifting Rocky high into the air and handing him over to Lars, Mia's bodyguard. 'We'll discuss that among ourselves at a later date, young man. For now I think you'd better be going, or you'll be late. Don't want to keep the crowd waiting.'

It was true! You could hear not only all the people screaming outside, but the music playing inside.

It was only RIGHT THEN that Mia noticed what Nishi and I and the rest of the bridesmaids and junior bridesmaids were wearing.

'Oh,' she said, appearing a bit startled. 'You're all in . . .'

'Purple!' I cried, twirling around in my dress, which, by the way, did not have any paw prints on it. 'Surprise! Grandmère did it! Well, Grandmère and I did it, together. I know you wanted cream-coloured dresses for your bridesmaids, but Grandmère and I thought you'd like this better, because purple is the colour of royalty, and for a wedding, it's different . . . like you!'

'Yeah,' Lilly muttered, looking down at her purple skirt. 'It's different, all right. Who cares if we look like aubergines?'

'Speak for yourself,' Perin said. She's the one bridesmaid who doesn't like to wear dresses, and Mia wanted all of her friends to feel comfortable, so Sebastiano made her a morning suit, like the groomsmen's, but with a purple tie. She looked very dashing in it.

'*I* love my dress,' Tina said fiercely. 'Purple is one of my favourite colours.'

'Mine, too,' Marguerite and Victorine chimed in.

'*I* look good in everything,' Luisa said. 'So I don't care.'

'*Everyone* looks good in purple,' Shameeka said. And Shameeka would know, since she works in fashion. 'Especially on a red carpet.'

'*I* think you all look amazing.' Mia's mom, who was wearing a dress that was a slightly different shade of purple than mine and Grandmère's, looked pretty amazing herself. 'But what matters is what Mia thinks. Mia, are *you* all right with it?'

We all looked anxiously at Mia.

'I . . .' Mia said, the corners of her mouth trembling. I couldn't tell if she was happy or sad. 'I . . .'

Oh no! She hated it! Grandmère had been wrong, and the wedding was ruined! Only not because of a mistake — that my dog got muddy paw prints all over my dress, or that Rocky had eaten the top of the wedding cake — but because of something I'd done on purpose (well, mostly Grandmère had done it, but I hadn't told her not to).

I felt terrible.

Then something amazing happened:

My sister burst out laughing! The same way she'd laughed at the RGA, after we'd finished performing 'All Roads Lead to Genovia'. It was almost like she was crying, she was laughing so hard. In fact, I was a little bit worried she was going to fall down, she was laughing so hard.

'Oh no,' I heard Ling Su whisper. 'The stress has finally got to her. She's cracking up.'

But then after a few seconds, Mia caught her breath, and, wiping tears from her eyes, said, 'No, no, I'm fine. Really. The purple is great. I love it. You're right, Olivia. Purple is the colour of royalty.'

Relief flooded through me — more even than when I'd woken up from my nightmare about Snowball and the paw prints and realized it had all been just a dream.

'You see?' Grandmère leaned down to whisper to

me, smiling in triumph. 'I told you. We saved this wedding.'

It was true! Grandmère's plan (whatever it was) worked!

Then my sister took each of her parents by the arm (after Paolo hurried over and redid her eyeliner, because it had become smeared when she cried), and turned towards the wide doors to the throne room. The music had grown louder. Soon, I knew, it would be our cue.

That's when I got nervous. It wasn't over yet! There was still a chance I could ruin everything. After all, Nishi and I still had a very important job to do. Mia's veil of handmade lace was impossibly delicate. If the weight of one very elderly cat could tear it, who knew what else could go wrong?

Plus, when I bent to lift it, I happened to notice Luisa standing nearby with Marguerite and Victorine. They looked as much like naiads as Nishi and me. Except that they didn't have tiaras, and I did.

Maybe it was the fact that Grandmère and I had

just made Mia cry with laughter right before her marriage to Michael. Maybe it was the music, or how beautiful my sister looked, or the sunlight, or all the sparkles. But suddenly, I was filled with love for everyone.

Even Luisa Ferrari.

'Luisa,' I said to her, overcome with emotion. 'We're cousins. But what I really want to be is friends. Let's not fight, OK? At least not today.'

Luisa smirked and rolled her eyes. 'Kee-yow, Olivia. Whatever you say.'

This wasn't exactly the reaction I'd been hoping for. But considering it was Luisa, it was enough.

And then we were standing outside the throne room, and I could hear all the people screaming outside the palace, and all the music inside, and knew:

This was it. It was the Big Moment.

'Everything's going to be all right,' Vivianne said, shoving flower baskets into Luisa's, Victorine's and Marguerite's hands. 'Remember, take it slow. There's no rush. We have all the time in the world.'

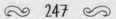

'We don't, actually,' Grandmère said. 'The television studio said to try to get it over with by the next commercial break.'

'Princess Clarisse,' Vivianne said, 'don't you need to take your seat? *Now*?'

Grandmère tossed her head, pulled Rommel close on his crystal leash, and disappeared.

Paolo walked over and pressed a tissue to Luisa's lips. 'What did I say to you yesterday about this? Less is more. Did I say this?'

Luisa tossed her own head. 'I don't remember.'

'I do. I remember.' Paolo looked at Mia. 'You look like an angel who fell down from heaven to be with us.'

She smiled. 'Don't exaggerate, Paolo.'

'Thank you,' he said. 'This is what you say when someone pays you a compliment, Your Highness. Thank you. Why can you never say thank you? So many years and still no thank you.' To Dad, he said, 'Too much bronzer. Someone fix the prince. Is this too much to ask?'

'Annnd,' Vivianne said, tapping her headset. 'Bridesmaids, take positions.'

I lifted Mia's train and was surprised by how much heavier the delicate handmade lace felt than the tablecloth she'd worn around her waist in yesterday's rehearsal. It had to weigh a ton!

I shot Nishi my 'OMG!' look but felt an even

bigger shock when I saw her face. She looked as if she was about to throw up.

'Nishi,' I whispered urgently. 'Are you all right?'

'I don't think so,' she whispered back. 'I'm so nervous. I . . . I don't know if I can do this.'

Uh-oh.

The truth was, I didn't know if I could do it, either.

But what choice did we have? We had to do it! For the people of Genovia, but more importantly, for my sister.

'Nishi. Of course you can! This is what you've always dreamed of!'

'Not this,' she whispered. 'I mean, yes, this, but I didn't think it would be like this.'

'Like what?' I looked around. 'This is EXACTLY what it's like. We're in beautiful dresses about to walk down the aisle of a throne room, and everyone is looking at us.'

'I know!' she cried. 'I don't think I can take the pressure.'

'All we have to do is hold the back of her dress,' I

said, nodding at my sister. 'How do you think SHE feels? She's the one getting married. All we have to do is help by not messing up.'

It was surprising how hard this was.

Beyond the throne room doors, I could hear the music swelling. Rocky was probably well on his way down the aisle with the rings.

'Are you ready?' I heard Dad murmur in front of us, but to Mia, not to us.

'Are you?' she replied, and squeezed his arm, smiling. 'Remember, you two aren't losing a daughter. You're gaining another member of the family business.'

This was a little joke. The family business is the Royal House of Renaldo. When Michael marries Mia, he has to take her last name. That's what royal consorts do.

'I think he'll make a fine addition,' Dad said, smiling back at her.

'I do, too,' Helen Thermopolis said.

'Look, if Rocky can do it,' I said to Nishi, 'we can. He's only nine.'

'I guess that's true.' She didn't look very reassured. 'But maybe we should let your cousin do it.' She nodded at Luisa, who was taking last-minute selfies with Marguerite and Victorine before Vivianne could confiscate their phones. 'She's had modelling experience.'

'Are you KIDDING me?' I couldn't believe what I was hearing. 'We can do this, Nishi. We're only carrying a skirt.'

'True,' Nishi said. 'But on international TV.'

It was pretty fortunate then that Mia turned to give us a dazzling smile. 'I'm so happy you're here,' she said. 'You're going to do great.'

Then Vivianne was saying, 'Bridesmaids! Go!'

Mia's friends began to walk, followed by Victorine, Marguerite and Luisa.

And suddenly my sister and Dad were moving, and I had no chance to feel nervous, because I was too busy making sure Mia's handmade lace veil and train stayed smooth and untangled, which really wasn't that easy, seeing how long they were and how fast she was moving — not slow like Vivianne had instructed her.

But when you're a bride — and a princess — you can do whatever you want. And I suppose I'd be in a hurry to get it over with, too, if I were getting married, so I could get to the cake quickly.

I had time to see that everyone on either side of the aisle had stood up and was smiling at us — well,

at my sister, probably, but some people were also smiling at me and Nishi — as we went by. The music — the blaring trumpets and harps of the Genovian national anthem — sounded like heaven, and the crystals on my sister's dress were still blazing like thousands of tiny diamonds in the sunlight streaming from the throne room windows.

Even though she was going so fast, it took a while to get down to the throne room to where the prime minister was waiting, but neither Nishi nor I messed up once (nor did anyone else. I didn't see a single flower petal out of place, or any wedding guests who might have been stabbed by Rocky's sword).

The only thing that WAS out of place was the expression on Michael's face when we finally reached him at the end of the throne room. It was a lot like how he'd looked after we'd finished our 'All Roads Lead to Genovia' performance — like he was trying not to cry.

Only I don't think he was crying with laughter this time, because there is definitely nothing funny about a Genovian wedding ceremony — no lederhosen or dirndls in sight. It's completely serious!

But I don't think he was sad, either, or scared. I think he was happy, the way all those people in the Great Hall had been when Mia came down the stairs, or the way Mia was when she saw us in our purple dresses. I think Michael thought she looked really, really beautiful.

And that made me want to cry with happiness, too.

Only I didn't have time, because I had a job to do. It's no joke being in charge of the bridal train. After the music ended and the prime minister asked everyone to be seated, Nishi and I had to make sure

Mia wasn't twisted up in her skirt and veil. In fact, *every time* she turned towards the prime minister or Michael, we had to do this, or she could have fallen over due to her legs having become tangled in her own clothing!

Genovian wedding ceremonies aren't like the ones you see on TV where the bride and groom promise to honour each other in sickness and in health. Instead, Genovian brides and grooms promise to:

- Stay true to the Genovian constitution and to each other
- Educate and feed their children
- Never hit each other, their children, or their livestock or pets
- Pay their taxes (even though in Genovia there are no taxes)
- Never throw fish heads into Genovian waters and pollute it, but dispose of them properly

(That last one is very controversial and people have been asking for it to be taken out of the traditional Genovian wedding service. But Mia and Michael asked that it be left in, since neither of them is religious, but they feel *some* traditions should be preserved, such as the careful disposal of fish heads.)

Even though I don't really like mushy stuff, I thought it was a very romantic ceremony. (I didn't cry, however, like Nishi did. Mia's and Michael's mothers cried, too, especially at the part about raising their children to be well-rounded Genovian citizens. Even Michael cried a little at that part, maybe because he was thinking about the twins, Han and Solo.)

But he looked very serious when the prime minister got to the part where they exchanged rings — which turned out OK, because Prince Khalil took charge of the ring pillow as soon as Rocky got to the front of the room. Good thing, too, since Rocky spent most of the ceremony playing around with his sword, even though his mom kept giving him the evil eye — when she wasn't crying, of course.

Then Michael had to pledge his loyalty to the country of Genovia, forsaking citizenship of all other nations so that he could be prince consort of Her Royal Highness Princess Amelia Mignonette Grimaldi Thermopolis Renaldo.

That's when he had to kneel in front of Mia and pledge his undying troth to her, the crown and the House of Renaldo.

Then she took a sword and laid it once on each of his shoulders and pronounced him her royal consort Prince Michael Renaldo of Genovia, and the prime minister declared that he could kiss his bride.

I thought Nishi was going to keel over with excitement, but I was so busy making sure Mia didn't get tangled up in her veil and train (and also keeping Rocky from pulling out his own sword, since he thought this was the part where everybody got to swordfight) that I missed when the two of them actually kissed . . .

But I hear it was very, very steamy! Nishi said that Michael picked Mia up! And that Michael's crown fell off (but Boris P caught it before it hit the dais).

Anyway, the next thing I knew, everyone was cheering, and the bride and groom were hurrying down the aisle to where the royal carriages were waiting outside to begin the parade that would take them — and all of us — around downtown Genovia, to wave at the populace, receive congratulations and have confetti thrown down on us from the upper windows of the quaint Genovian cottages and shops.

Which I have to say was quite fun, except that Mia was right about one thing: purple really *is* quite hot in Genovia in summertime!

Especially in an open-air carriage in the noonday sun, even when everyone is spraying champagne everywhere.

But I'm not going to complain, because I'm the one who suggested it.

Well, me and Grandmère.

I can sort of see why Luisa is changing before tonight's ball.

But I'm not going to. Because here is a secret:

Just now, when we got back from the parade and were standing around here in the throne room getting our photos taken (yes! We had to come back after the parade to get wedding photos, which is how I've had the time to write this. It's *so* boring!), Prince Khalil came up to tell me I look 'very nice' in my dress and tiara.

I was surprised.

Not that I like him or anything (except as a friend).

But that was very sweet of him. He didn't have to say I look nice.

That's not why I'm never changing out of this dress again. I just don't want to, that's all.

Hmmmm . . . I wonder if Grandmère knew all along that purple is the colour that looks best on me, and this was all part of her plan, or —

Got to go. More royal wedding photos. Honestly, the work of being a princess never ends.

Sunday 21 June
Noon
Royal Genovian Bedroom
Day After the Royal Wedding

EEEEEEEEEEEEEEEEEEEEEEEEEEEEEE
EEEEEEEEEEEEEEEEEEEEEEEEEEEEEE
EEEEEEEEEEEEEEEE!!!!!!!!!!!!!!!!!!!!!!!!!!!!!!!!!!

Last night was the best night of my life!!!!!!

I did change out of my dress. I had to, because Francesca, my wardrobe consultant, made me. She said everyone was going to be changing into evening-wear for the ball, so I had to, too.

I told her I couldn't change because purple is my good-luck colour, and I didn't have anything else purple, much less anything as fancy as what I knew Luisa would be wearing — her Claudio evening gown with the detachable skirt.

But Francesca said, 'Here,' and handed me something. It was a large box with a bow on it.

I said, 'What's this?'

'It's from your sister,' Francesca said. 'It's your bridesmaid gift.'

'Bridesmaid gift?' I echoed. 'What's a bridesmaid gift?'

'It's the gift the bride and groom give to members of their wedding party, to show their appreciation for your support.'

My support? Well, I *have* been pretty supportive. Keeping that train and veil from getting tangled was very, very difficult!

But when I opened the box, I saw that Mia and Michael — or Prince Michael, as I suppose I should call him now — had gone *way* too far. Inside was a top made all over of sequins, with a big floaty wraparound skirt.

'*Oh!*' I cried, even though as a general rule, I'm

not a fan of dresses that are too girly (unless they're for weddings, of course).

But it wasn't a dress. It was *a skirt and top*. Even better, the top was a *swimsuit*. A one-piece swimsuit *made of sequins*.

'Yes,' Francesca said, not looking too happy about it. Francesca doesn't approve of swimsuits with sequins on them. I know, because I've asked her for a sequinned swimsuit about a million times, but she's always said the same thing: *Sequinned swimsuits are inappropriate for young royals*. Obviously Mia didn't agree! 'They consulted me about the size. There is a note. Perhaps you should read it.'

I found the note and read it.

From the Desk of HRH Amelia Renaldo of Genovia

Dear Olivia
Michael and I want to thank you for everything you've done to help make our wedding so wonderful. You've been so cheerful, patient, and kind even when I know you weren't feeling that way.

We especially want to thank you for the drawing you made of us, which I found under my door this morning. It's beautiful. I'm going to have it framed and hung over the babies' cribs, so they'll always be able to see it, and think of us, and of you.

You're the best sister — and will be the best aunt — anyone could ever have. But most of all you're a true princess.

Love,

Mia

I couldn't believe it! This is the best letter I've ever got in my life.

I'm so glad I tore that drawing I made of her and Michael from my notebook and slid it under her door this morning (after I found out that her wedding cake got destroyed).

That's not the only reason I did it, of course . . . it was the only thing I could think of to give them as a wedding present, since I don't have any money, and the performance of 'All Roads Lead to Genovia' didn't really seem like that good of a gift. It was a gift from the entire school, not from *me*.

But people like things you make — at least if you do a decent job. It's *always* good to give people you love something from your heart.

I was especially happy that Mia and Michael had liked my gift enough to give me a gift in return, one I'd especially wanted . . . until I found out a few minutes later that Nishi had got *the exact same gift*.

Then I was ECSTATIC. Because it meant that Mia really, really understood me!

'Can we wear them to the reception?' Nishi and I asked Francesca, who looked very pained when Nishi burst into my room wearing her gift and started jumping up and down, screaming.

'If you must,' Francesca said. 'Apparently that was the idea.'

'It's like your sister *knew* about us being naiads,' Nishi kept saying, dancing around and around in her sequined bathing suit and floaty skirt. 'It's like she's *psychic*.'

'I think it was her friend Shameeka,' I said. 'Or Lana. They know more about this stuff. But whoever. It doesn't matter. Because we look *amazing*.'

I was so happy! I didn't think I could be happier.

But I was wrong.

Because after we went down to the party, and Princess Komiko and Queen Amina and all the other people from school began to arrive, and Boris P came out on to the stage and began to play, Nishi and I forgot all about our swimsuit-naiad dresses and started having the *best time at a wedding reception* we have ever had in our lives.

(Well, actually, for me it was the first time I have ever been to a wedding reception. But it was still the best time!)

Chef Bernard made lobster mac and cheese so there would be enough food to go around, and also added mini grilled-cheese sandwiches with tomato soup in cocktail glasses, and this turned out to be exactly what Mia and Michael had wanted in the first place, but Grandmère said it wouldn't be elegant enough for a royal wedding.

So they were super happy!

And Lilly's suggestion, having tables and chairs outside in the garden and by the pool, was just perfect, because all the old people, like the baroness and Grandmère and the world leaders, sat in the ballroom at the banquet tables in the air-conditioning, while the young people had a party outside . . . which is much better, if you ask me.

Out at the kids' party, Boris P was playing, and we were dancing and having fun.

But of course we weren't dancing the way Luisa had hoped there'd be dancing — no one held each other in the moonlight under the swaying Genovian palm fronds. No one danced together at all . . . well, except when we sang 'All Roads Lead to Genovia', which we did *one* final time, for my sister's sake, because Michael begged us to, as a special favour. I have never heard people applaud so much!

I don't know what it is about that song.

But that was the last time I'll ever have to sing it, thank goodness. And thank goodness, too, that no one could locate Prince Gunther at the time we performed it, so I only had to promenade with Rocky, and not the bogey-flinging Flexer (although to be fair, Prince Gunther doesn't fling bogeys any more, or flex that much, either).

There were a *couple* of dances that people did together. Mia and Michael did a first dance as a married couple to some old song that no one had ever heard of (or not me, anyway). Everyone stood around and watched and clapped. It was very nice.

And then Mia and Dad did a father-daughter dance, and Michael and his mom did a mother-son dance.

Then everyone started dancing to Boris P, but in a big group, not in couples or anything. The boys took their jackets off, and we girls took our shoes off, and we all started jumping around, acting crazy, trying not to fall in the pool. It was *so fun*.

Well, fun for everyone except Luisa. Not that she fell in the pool (which would have been hilarious). She just wouldn't dance, not even when Victorine or Marguerite or I tried to pull her on to the dance floor. She said we were being 'immature' and 'didn't know anything'.

Then, when I brought her a tomato soup cocktail and a mini grilled cheese, because I thought maybe her problem was that she was just hungry and sad because her parents hadn't come to the wedding on account of hating being in the same country together, she didn't even say thank you. She said, 'You and your friend look stupid in those matching dresses.' She meant Nishi, who was dancing in a big group with Rocky, Princess Komiko and a bunch of other people. 'In case you didn't know.'

'Really?' I felt mad, but also kind of like laughing. She was just such a . . . Luisa Ferrari. 'They aren't dresses. They're swimsuits, with skirts.'

'Well, that's even stupider,' Luisa said. 'This is a royal ball, not a swim meet.'

I shook my head. Luisa couldn't hurt my feelings any more, I realized, partly because of what Grandmère said, and partly because . . . well, I'm a true princess now! My sister said so.

And even if I weren't, I wouldn't care what she said. She's Luisa Ferrari. She has no power over me.

Which is good, because when she finds out what I heard my sister tell Madame Alain over by the chocolate fountain — that in the fall, all the schools in Genovia, including the RGA, will be required by royal proclamation to make room for refugee children, or face fines and even closure — Luisa is going to *plotz* (*plotz* means drop dead from surprise. I learned it from Michael's mom).

I don't doubt this idea was cooked up by my grandmother in order to teach the Ferraris to have more character. I saw Grandmère over by the chocolate fountain as my sister and Madame Alain were speaking. I'm positive she planted the notion in my sister's head . . .

But that doesn't mean it's a bad one. In fact, I think it's a good one. Going to school with a bunch of non-royals is going to be very challenging for my cousin . . .

And very educational, as well. A lot like it's been for me, going to school with a bunch of royals.

'Here, Luisa,' I said, handing her a piece of wedding cake. 'You look like you need this.'

'Are you kidding me?' She stared at it in horror. 'I don't eat *cake*.'

'Why not? It's a wedding. It's bad luck not to eat the cake.'

'Fine.' She made a face but took the cake from me and started eating it. 'But if I burst out of this dress, I'm going to make your dad pay for it. This is a *Claudio*. Not that anyone at this party has noticed. Least of all *him*.' She stabbed her fork in Prince Khalil's direction. He'd taken off his tuxedo jacket, too, along with all the other boys, and was dancing away to one of Boris P's biggest hits, 'A Million Stars', which Boris was singing to Mia's friend Tina, with whom he'd got back together, much to everyone's relief. It turned out that he hadn't cheated, after all.

I tried not to notice that Prince Khalil looked very, very cute.

'I don't think boys like Prince Khalil care about designers,' I said as politely as I could.

Luisa made another face. 'I suppose not. If I were wearing an *iguana*, he'd care.'

It was kind of a bummer sitting next to Luisa. But since I was one of the hostesses of the reception, I felt like I couldn't just leave her there, feeling so sad, because that wouldn't be very princessy.

And of course I remembered what Grandmère had said about how it was our duty as royals to guide those who were less fortunate . . . which is kind of funny, in a weird way, since Luisa had been assigned to me as *my* guide, at the RGA! But now there I was, guiding her. Or trying to, anyway.

But then — just like with my bridesmaid gift from Mia — suddenly I was rewarded for all my hard work when something *amazing* happened.

'Princess Olivia?' a voice called from the darkness.

And from the garden beyond the strands of fairy lights the gardeners and I had placed between the palm trees stepped a figure I didn't recognize — though later I realized I *should* have, since it was a boy I knew. He had very big arms and shoulders — made to look even bigger by the oversize tuxedo he was wearing — an Austrian accent, and hair so blond that it was almost gold . . .

'P-Prince Gunther!' I stammered, standing up. 'Your . . . your hair. It isn't green any more!'

'Oh, yah,' he said, bashfully running his fingers through his now yellow mane. 'This was the surprise I texted you about.'

Luisa stood up, too. Her jaw was hanging open. 'Prince Gunther, you look *amazing*.'

'*Danke*,' he said. 'You do, too. Is that a Claudio?'

Luisa looked down at herself in astonishment. 'What . . . *what* did you say?'

'I asked if that was a Claudio.' Gunther strolled up to us and pointed at Luisa's dress. 'I know that designer. My mother likes him very much. She used to be a model for him. She has had everything in his collections for the past ten years. She especially likes his resort wear, for when we go to Majorca at Fronleichnam.'

I thought Luisa might *plotz* with surprise. 'My mom loves Claudio's resort wear, too.'

I had no idea what the two of them were talking about, but as the hostess of this part of the party, I thought it was my duty to ask, 'Prince Gunther. What happened to you? Where have you been?'

'Oh, I'm sorry I'm late, Princess,' he said. 'The lemon juice I used to get the green out of my hair took longer than I thought. Please will you accept my apologies, and also give them to the bride and groom?'

'Uh,' I said. 'Sure.' I had no idea where Mia and Michael were. It was late, and I hadn't seen them in hours. For all I knew, they might have gone to bed. I couldn't blame them. They'd been smiling so much all day for the photographers, so I could imagine they were both probably exhausted.

Suddenly now Luisa was smiling, too.

'Is *that* a Claudio?' she asked, pointing at Prince Gunther's tuxedo.

'Uh, yes,' Gunther said. 'It is vintage. It belonged to my grandfather.'

Luisa sucked in her breath. 'Vintage? Do you know how much a vintage Claudio tuxedo is worth?'

'Yes,' Prince Gunther said. 'My father would kill me if he knew I was wearing it. But I figured, for an occasion like this, it would be worth it—'

The next thing I knew, Luisa was pulling Prince Gunther down on to a chair at her table and grilling him about his mother's Claudio collection.

And Prince Gunther didn't seem to mind, although he looked very nervous. In a *good* way.

I couldn't believe it. Luisa wasn't showing off in front of a boy to get attention, *or* being mean to him (or me, or anyone else). She was simply having a conversation with another person about something in which she was interested . . . and that person was interested in it, too!

I wasn't sure if this proved she was finally showing character or common sense, but it seemed to show that *I'd* done my duty as a good hostess. I slowly began to back away, feeling a sense of satisfaction . . .

. . . when suddenly my hand was seized, and someone started tugging on it.

And it turned out to be the last person in the world I ever expected: PRINCE KHALIL.

'Olivia,' he said urgently, dragging me around the edge of the pool. 'I'm so glad I found you. Come here, quick!'

I didn't know what was happening — I thought maybe Mia and Michael were leaving for their honeymoon, and we were all supposed to go and wave goodbye. Or maybe the fireworks were starting, or I was needed for a special photo op with the queen of England or Boris P or something.

But it wasn't any of those things! Instead, Prince Khalil steered me towards the orange tree beneath my bedroom window — where it was was pretty dark, considering it was night-time and none of us had thought to place any fairy lights there — and pointed.

'Look!' he cried.

I looked, but all I saw was that they'd forgotten to take away one of the live traps. Then, inside it, I noticed the faintest hint of movement . . .

An iguana! Not just any iguana, though. A bright green baby iguana.

I gasped. 'Carlos!'

Khalil looked at me curiously. 'Carlos? Who's Carlos?'

'Um,' I said. 'No one.' I didn't want him to know I'd named one of the iguanas. That was probably a violation of the Genovian Herpetology Rescue Society code of ethics or something.

'I just wanted to show you that we missed one,' Prince Khalil said. 'I hope your grandmother won't feel as if we failed her. I'm sure it's the last one. I'll come by in the morning and pick it up, if you want.'

'No,' I said quickly, before I could stop myself. 'Please don't! That's Carlos.'

Even though it was dark beneath the orange tree,

the moon had begun to peek out from above the palace walls, so I could see his face clearly enough to tell that he was baffled. 'Wait . . . you have a *pet iguana*?'

'Well, not really a pet,' I said, feeling embarrassed. 'He just hangs out here.' I pointed at the window above us, trying to figure out how to explain it. 'That's my bedroom, you see? I guess I've got . . . well, used to him. I'd miss him if he was moved to the golf course. Wouldn't it be all right for us to keep just one? I'm sure my grandmother wouldn't mind. Carlos is like family now.'

Slowly, Prince Khalil smiled. 'Wow. I never thought I'd meet a girl who likes iguanas . . . let alone a *princess*. I thought princesses only liked dresses and things.'

'Oh,' I said uncomfortably, thinking of Luisa. 'Well, you can be a princess and like lots of different things. Dresses, drawing, football, horseback riding, ruling the country and, uh, iguanas. Though to be honest, I didn't really like iguanas at first. But once I got to know them, they sort of grew on me.'

I realized I wasn't only talking about iguanas . . .

I was talking about the RGA . . . and my cousin Luisa . . . and maybe even Prince Khalil!

That made me feel even *more* uncomfortable, especially because of the way he kept staring at me. Why did his eyes have to be so brown?

'And anyway,' I added, 'isn't that your job?'

He was still staring at me like I had something on my face. 'Isn't what my job?'

'Isn't it part of your job with the Herpetology Society to educate the public about how it's good to have reptiles and amphibians around? Because they're beneficial to the environment?'

'Oh, yes,' he said, and smiled some more. 'Exactly.'

'So maybe,' I said, 'we could keep just one. This one. Carlos.'

'Definitely,' he said. 'I can show you how to take care of him and what to feed him and stuff. I could come over anytime if you want, because my parents will be staying here in Genovia for the summer.'

'Oh,' I said. 'That would be great.'

Then when he showed me how to open the live trap to let Carlos go (although of course the dumb thing was asleep, or scared or something, and wouldn't leave, so we practically had to shake the cage up and down to get him to go), Prince Khalil accidentally put his hand over mine while I was trying to work the latch.

'Oops,' he said, and smiled some more. 'Sorry.'

'That's OK,' I said, and smiled back. I don't know what was wrong with me. I wasn't feeling uncomfortable any more. I couldn't stop smiling!

Especially when we were making our way back to the party — Prince Khalil had closed the door to the live trap so Carlos couldn't go back in there and promised to come by tomorrow (which is today) to get it — and he asked, 'Hey, do you want to dance?'

'Sure,' I said. Because I had no idea what was going on. I think in this one area, Luisa might be right. I *AM* a dumb, immature little baby. 'I've been dancing all night. Didn't you see me?'

'No,' he said, looking as embarrassed as I was about to feel. 'I meant with me. Do you want to dance with me?'

At first I wasn't sure if what I heard was in my head or my heart, but it sounded like a *million* firecrackers going off at the same time, exploding in the air and causing a burst of light that blazed even brighter than the crystals on my sister's wedding dress.

And that's because the royal wedding fireworks display *had* started going off right at that very moment, just above our heads, in huge eruptions of Genovian white, green and blue.

With my heart slamming in my chest, I said, 'Why, yes, Prince Khalil, I would *love* to dance with you.'

So we did!

Not a slow dance or anything.

But we definitely danced under the moonlight and by the fountain! We even touched hands once, when I almost lost my balance and would have slipped into the pool if he hadn't reached out, laughing, and saved me!

It was *amazing*.

I still haven't stopped smiling. And that's because I've finally realized something: I think Nishi might be right.

Prince Khalil *does* like me! As more than just a friend. And guess what else?

I think I like him, too. ☺

I guess this wedding didn't turn out to be a disaster after all. And I haven't turned out to be such a disaster at this princess thing, either!

Well, I'd better go to bed now. With Mia leaving for her honeymoon, I'm going to have a *lot* more responsibilities around here starting tomorrow. Like Grandmère says, every woman needs at least eight hours of sleep a night so that she can wake refreshed upon the morning to battle the new day.

Genovia

By Olivia Grace

A Olivia's Room
B Grandmère's Room
C Mia's Room
D Rocky's Room
E Main Staircase
F Throne Room
G Ballroom
H Billiard Room
I Dad's Office
J Hall of Portraits
K Kitchens
L Royal Dining Room
M Royal Genovian Guards
N Library
O Tennis Courts
P Stables
Q Royal Genovian Gardens
R Royal Genovian Academy
S Downtown Genovia
T Beach
U Royal Genovian Yacht Club